GW00775762

 **Library and Information Service**

Library materials must be returned on or before the last due date or fines will be charged at the current rate. Items can be renewed by telephone, email or by visting the website, letter or personal call unless required by another borrower. For hours of opening and charges see notices displayed in libraries.
Tel: 03333 704700
Email: libraries@lewisham.gov.uk
www.lewisham.gov.uk/libraries

915 00000176047

ISBN: 1985136198
ISBN-13: 978-1985136199

# DEDICATION

For my parents who walked this path together.

# ACKNOWLEDGMENTS

Michelle Arnold – My grammar and typo savior!

Kelly Daniel – My medical advisor.

My family and friends – Their continued support and encouragement knows no bounds.

My fellow Lesfic authors who selflessly help to promote and encourage a newbie to the scene.

And My Wife – Whose love is never-ending.

# Part One

Claire Highton-Stevenson

Chapter One

Cancer. That was what the doctor had said little more than a minute earlier - it was cancer. They thought they had prepared themselves for such an outcome, in as much as you can prepare with hopeful words and pamphlets as your only guide on what to expect. The doctors had been optimistic, but the warning had been there all the same: to prepare for the worst, hope for the best.

Stage 4. That was what the doctor had said next. It had spread, ferociously, aggressive. The liver and the brain. A malignant outcome was always a possibility, but they had talked only of beating it - assuming stage 2 at the very worst. Staying positive and hoping for the best had been the only course of action.

Now, it was worse than the worst.

Terminal. The doctor has said a lot of words in the few minutes they had sat across the desk from her, and yet only a few of them had managed to penetrate, settle, and be acknowledged. Terminal and incurable, treatments.

"How long?" One of them had finally addressed the elephant in the room out loud, and the doctor had paused to look through her notes. The paper shuffling was loud in the silence of the clinically white office. She already knew the answer. It was a stalling tactic, because it didn't matter how often she did this; it never got any easier.

"It's difficult to quantify, with the right treatments some women have gone on to live for several years." She saw the hope in the partner's blue eyes. "However, the likelihood is much less."

Those blue eyes clouded once more, trying desperately to keep the tears unshed, to be strong and hold it all together.

The walls felt like they were closing in. The doctor was speaking again, passing over more leaflets with information for them to read later when it had 'sunk in' a little more. Sunk in? She was going to die, what more was there to 'sink in?'

~***~

They stood quickly, chairs scraping against the floor. Hands reached out to shake as they both thanked the doctor - for what exactly?

The long walk back to the car was unhurried, and in the grand scheme of things, it wasn't something they needed to rush. Not today.

Susan climbed into the passenger seat and sat quietly waiting for Ali to get in too. It had probably hit Ali harder than Susan, even though it was Susan with the prognosis. Susan was the stronger of the two. She was the organiser, the one that made sure birthday cards were sent on time and anniversaries were celebrated. It would be Susan who anyone called with bad news because Ali would just get upset and not know what to do, but Susan always knew. She thought back to the day just two weeks ago when their world had been turned on its head.

*They had just made love, and it had been tender and frantic all at the same time. They were lying together on the bed, their bed, that they had brought with them the day they had moved in. The marital bed they had shared for almost eight years. Susan was lying on her back, resting on the pillow, catching her breath. Her left arm was pushed up behind her head as she held Ali tucked up into her right-hand side, the fingers of her wife lazily stroking her left breast as they talked about everything and nothing.*

*At first, Ali had passed over it, barely noticing, but the second time she had felt it she had sat up, balanced on her elbow as she grew more serious.*

*"What is it?" Susan had asked, noticing the change in her wife's demeanour.*

*"I'm not sure, probably nothing, but I think there's a lump." Her fingers skimmed back and forth, pressing harder until she located it again, and Susan too had felt it.*

*"I think you're right, I'll call Doctor Sorenson first thing in the morning. Don't worry love, it will probably just be a cyst, a sign I am getting old." She chuckled, but the laughter didn't reach her eyes, and Ali still worried.*

"We're going to fight this, right?" Ali said, looking straight ahead and out of the windscreen. She kept her gaze on the meandering of other people climbing in and out of cars as they made their way to and from appointments.

"Yes, of course," Susan had replied, her voice quiet, but her words firm enough that Ali chanced a glimpse. She didn't want to look, knew that if she spent too long looking at her wife it would break her and she would be of no use, but she couldn't look away and pretend her wife wasn't sitting right next to her, fighting for her life.

She nodded to herself and turned the key in the ignition, slipping the car into drive and slowly moving out of the parking space. She took them home.

Chapter Two

Walking into the house together it all felt so normal, like nothing had changed. The cat from next door still greeted them on the path that led up to the door. Ali still bent down and tickled his chin, rubbing his ears as he twisted his head in her palm. The smell of lavender permeated the garden from the pots that sat on the porch. Everything was exactly how it should be.

Only it wasn't.

Susan opened the door and walked in first, like she always did. They both entered the open-planned kitchen that had taken over six months to plan and let out the breaths they had been holding in. Ali flicked the switch on the kettle as Susan tipped a spoonful of instant coffee into two cups and left them for Ali to finish while she wandered upstairs and got changed into something more comfortable.

~***~

Sitting down gently on the end of the bed with a sigh, she studied herself in the mirror. The image reflecting back at her was almost mocking: green eyes clouding a little with unshed tears. She didn't look ill. She looked just the way she had done six months ago; a year even. Ok, her blonde hair was a little longer, but she couldn't say that she looked like someone with cancer, let alone someone who was dying.

She was dying.

She sighed deeply and stood, opening the mahogany door to the wardrobe. She hung her jacket, stripped off her remaining clothes, and crossed the room. Everything was where it should be. The drawer slid open and she pulled on a pair of Ali's sweats, tying them at the waist before she added one of her t-shirts too.

Susan took the stairs slowly. It was only a short flight of ten steps that led straight into the living room, and yet it felt like twice as many. Her coffee sat on a coaster, one of the comedy ones they had picked up on a trip to Vegas the year before. She smiled at the memory.

"Ali?" she called out. She had expected to find her wife sitting in her usual chair drinking her own coffee. The room was empty, as was the kitchen. The door to the back garden was ajar and she walked slowly towards it, her eyes drawn to the window set in the centre of the painted wood.  Ali sat on the floor, her back to the wall of the house with her knees pulled up tight to her chin, her arms wrapped firmly around them. Her long, dark hair covered her face, which was buried in the small space on top of her knees as her thin shoulders shook uncontrollably.

Susan stood in the doorway. She wanted to go to her, comfort her, pull her into her arms making promises she couldn't keep, but she knew her wife. She knew that she wouldn't cry in front of her, she would bottle it all up and hold it in, so she left her to cry.

~***~

In the small hours of the morning, when the darkness had eclipsed everything, they made love. Ali had tenderly taken Susan in her arms, her kisses gentle and sweet. As they explored each other, Susan couldn't help but notice Ali's avoidance of her breasts.

"Touch me," she whispered, taking Ali's strong hand and placing her palm against the underside of her breast.

"I don't want to hurt you," she whispered back. Not since the first time they slept together had Susan heard such uncertainty in Ali. It felt like that first night when every touch had been a first, when they were shy with each other and unsure what they should do.

"You could never hurt me. Touch me." And with those words of wisdom Ali worshipped her, made love to every inch of her body and allowed her to reciprocate with the undying feeling of love emanating from them both.

Chapter Three

Susan and Ali Jenkins had their whole lives mapped out. They had vacations planned, were discussing an extension to the house, and were looking into adoption. Everything was now on hold. The hospital had called and Susan was booked for surgery to remove the tumour in her breast and to assess the other areas that the cancer had spread to. She would then begin a course of chemotherapy in the hope that it would help to slow the growth and therefore give them more time.

Time was a word that used to mean so much more: time to plan and organise the things they wanted to do, wanted to see. Now what did time mean? Time to talk, say the things they needed to say. Pray, hope for the best, a miracle. How much time? For Ali, eternity wouldn't be enough time.

~***~

The television was on and Ali could hear the sound of laughter; not just a light chuckle of humour, but a real hearty howl of laughter. The sound brought a smile to her own face as she neared the living room and found her wife stretched out on the couch with tears streaming down her face, her nose crinkled, and her hand held fast to her chest as the characters on the screen continued to tickle her humour.

Slapstick comedy had always entertained Susan. Ali watched quietly from the doorway. On the screen, one of the characters fell over a paint pot, knocking it over in the process, which meant one of the other characters slipped and landed on his backside. Once more Susan shrieked out loud and wiped her eyes.

It was in that moment that she caught sight of her dark-haired wife, her smouldering good looks just as arousing now as they had always been. Susan's eyes smiled as she stared across the room, the upturn of her lips suggesting a smirk; she always did love it when she found herself in a room full of people and when she glanced around, she would find Ali's eyes searching her out too. They would lock on and she would give her that trademark smirk. The one that said, 'you're all mine'.

She sat up and patted the cushion of the couch beside her. Ali didn't need to be asked twice, and she swanned across the room gracefully before plonking down quickly, just in case anyone else tried to sneak in first.

"Hi," she said, leaning in to kiss Susan's cheek.

"I'm only getting cheek kisses now?" she pouted, then puckered up her lips, waiting. She didn't wait long before the feeling of warm lips pressed against her own. "Better."

Susan twisted around and lay back against Ali's side, her wife's arm raising and falling around her instantly. The rest of the day was spent lying together on the couch watching old movies and just being together.

~***~

"Have you got everything you need?" Ali asked from the doorway of their room as Susan zipped up the small case she would take to the hospital. It was the same small case they used whenever they went on vacation; it had been all over the world with them.

"I think so, I guess I don't really need much, it's only a couple of days and you can always bring anything I have forgotten." She smiled, a sad smile. She wasn't sad for herself. No, she was sad for Ali, watching her wife trying not to fall apart.

"Ok, let's go then, sooner we get there the sooner they can get you fixed," she said hurriedly, as she grabbed the case from the bed.

"Ali?" Susan whispered, but her wife pretended to not hear her. "Ali?" she said louder now, watching her wife come to a halt with her back still turned to her. "Darling, they can't fix me. This isn't going to make it go away." Her eyes filled with tears as she walked closer to her wife and held her, arms wrapping around her slim waist, her warm cheek rested on her back.

"I know," came the whispered reply.

~***~

The hospital room was bright and airy, with lots of natural light that came in through a large window to the left of the bed. The surgery had gone well, as well as could be expected anyway.

Ali sat in the uncomfortable chair by her wife's bed as she slept off the sedatives. Nurses came and went, reading charts and making notes. They offered her a cup of coffee, but she declined. She was nauseous.

Watching her sleep, she looked so peaceful, and it was a struggle for Ali to imagine that her wife was even sick, let alone dying. Her blonde hair fanned out on the pillow and shimmered in the late afternoon sunlight. Ali loved Susan's hair: running her fingers through it as they lay on the couch watching TV, grasping fistfuls of it as they made love, watching it blow in the wind as they walked along the shore. She would lose her hair, Ali surmised. Because of the chemo, Susan would lose all of her beautiful hair. Ali dreaded the thought of it because then it would be real, then Susan would look sick, would look like she was dying, and there would be no way Ali could pretend otherwise.

Chapter Four


Ali Jenkins was a successful graphic designer. She had built her company from scratch, started at the bottom and worked her way towards where she was today. They were comfortable financially and thankfully had a great health insurance, so everything that Susan would need would be available to her. She had a huge project on at the moment, but she was delegating her staff to deal with it. Usually, she would work all the hours there were to get something like this finished but now, now she hadn't even given it a thought.

Working so hard had meant that Susan could stay at home, run the house and organise their lives. It had meant that when the time came and they could adopt that Susan would be the stay-at-home parent. Ali loved nothing more than coming home from a hard day at work to find her wife pottering about in the kitchen, cooking up a storm. They had more time for each other since Susan stopped working and their relationship had gone from strength to strength. She couldn't imagine it any other way now, and yet she was going to have to eventually.

~***~

When Susan was awake and feeling a little more comfortable, the doctor reappeared with the prognosis. It was good news in that they had managed to remove everything from the breast.

They would start a course of chemo in the next few weeks, but the scans showed that where the cancer had spread to the brain, it would be a little more difficult. They could and would operate, but there was a good chance they wouldn't be able to remove it, and its position could cause far more issues for Susan by taking it out than by leaving it and trying to shrink it.

They talked for over an hour, questions flying back and forth as the doctor explained things Ali had no real understanding of.

~***~

When Susan arrived home from the hospital, the house was immaculate. Ali had never been the housewife type; cleaning was something she didn't even consider needed doing. It was usually Susan who kept the house looking nice. There were flowers sitting in the crystal vase her mother had given them on their wedding day, a wonderful bouquet of pinks and orange; Susan's favourite colours.

"I see someone has been busy in my absence," Susan playfully chuckled as Ali followed in behind her. The case in her hand had now grown to several bags of medication, and there was even a 'get well' balloon trailing in the air behind her, a gift from Ali's colleagues.

"Uh yeah, I figured you, uh—" She found herself stumbling over her words a lot lately, fearful to say the wrong thing. 'You won't be up to it' was what she wanted to say of course, but the finality of it and what it meant long term stopped her.

"Thank you, I guess there is hope for you yet." Susan smiled; she had a beautiful smile, Ali thought. She needed to see it more often.

"So, dinner? Are you hungry?" Ali asked, quickly changing the subject because there was no hope.

She watched as Susan took a seat on the couch and swung her feet up. She looked tired.

"No, not really," she sighed. "Maybe a light snack, just to tide me over," she said as she began to get up.

"Hey, uh-uh. You stay right where you are, I got this," she said, walking back to the kitchen. The large living area melded into the dining area along with the kitchen into one giant elegant room. From the comfortable cream-coloured couch, Susan could see Ali as she moved around the kitchen finding the ingredients she needed. They had always been so careful in the things they ate and drank. Trying to keep a healthy diet had been important to them both. It was ironic now though, as she watched Ali butter two slices of bread and build a sandwich to beat all sandwiches.

"Chicken salad with light mayo and mustard," she said, presenting the beautifully made sandwich with a flourish. "Just the way you like it."

"Thank you," Susan said, placing the plate on her lap. Ali stood over her like an expectant mother waiting for her to eat. She picked up the half nearest her and took a bite. "Mm, delicious."

She held Ali's gaze. They needed to talk, but somehow the words wouldn't come.

It had never been difficult in the past. They had always been able to communicate even if it meant an argument, but now, now there was this colossal elephant in the room that neither of them knew how to talk about.

She patted the seat next to her and lifted her legs to indicate Ali should sit, which she did. She lowered her legs back down and into Ali's lap; trapping her in place. Ali gently placed her hands on her shins.

"I don't want anyone to wear black," Susan announced as she took another bite of her sandwich. She watched Ali as she sucked in a breath. She hadn't been expecting that for a conversation starter and to be honest, neither had Susan, but there it was, as good a place as any to begin. "And I don't want flowers, only a bouquet from you. I would prefer that donations be made in my name to the cancer research fund." Ali was still yet to acknowledge she had spoken, her eyes glued firmly to her hands and her long, dark hair curtaining her face from view. "I want you to celebrate my life."

"Stop, just stop," Ali whispered. Susan put her plate down on the floor beside her and reached for Ali's hand.

"We need to discuss it."

"No, we don't. I don't want to." Ali spoke the words like a child that didn't want to go to school. Her heart broke anytime she thought of a life without Susan.

"Sweetheart, we need to—"

"No!" she shouted. "No, we don't need to do anything, they said you have years so—"

"Ali, please." She squeezed her hand. "You know that isn't true."

"Yes, yes, it is. Dr Meyer said so." Her face contorted with the effort not to cry. Susan reached out and cupped her cheek.

"Ali, Dr Meyer said that in some cases, but not in mine." Her words were gentle, soft and understanding. Ali looked at her now. "The tumour in my brain probably isn't operable."

"That's...that isn't what she said." Ali was desperate to win the point.

"Ali?" She waited for her to look at her once more. "You have to accept that I am going to die."

"No." She gently lifted Susan's legs and raced from the house. Susan heard the car start and the sound of the wheels screeching off of the driveway. She knew this would be difficult. She was the organiser, the practical one who would take the facts and work with them. Ali was always the dreamer. It was what made her so good at what she did. She could imagine and bring things to life, but she lived in denial whenever anything serious needed to be done, and that was fine because Susan would always deal with it. But she couldn't deal with this. She couldn't organise or fix this for Ali.

Chapter Five

When Susan began her chemotherapy, Ali took several days off from work to be at home with her. She had a good base of employees. They all understood the situation and were willing to step up if need be, which she was thankful for. She had wanted to be at home all the time, but Susan had put her foot down to that idea.

"Why?" Susan had asked when Ali suggested taking the time off.

"What do you mean why?" Ali bit back, incredulous.

"I mean, and don't take this the wrong way darling but, no. You will drive me crazy." She smirked.

"Oh that's just—" Ali was actually speechless. "Well fine, cook your own dinners." She smiled and the pair of them burst into laughter. Susan placed her arms around Ali's neck and kissed her lips.

"When I need help, I want to get a nurse." She watched Ali frown, hurt by the fact that Susan didn't want her. "Because," she began to explain quickly to put a stop to the doubts and pained look on her wife's face, "I want us to be as normal as we can be, and—" She raised a finger and placed it on Ali's soft lips when she was about to interrupt, "I don't want your memories of me being that of someone that can't—"

"Susan?" Ali whispered.

"No Ali, I don't want—"

"Susan, in sickness and in health remember?" Ali stroked a finger down her cheek and wiped away the solitary tear with the pad of her thumb. She had never gotten used to seeing her wife cry. She hated it and would do anything to change it.

"I don't want you to remember me this way."

"Let's worry about it when the time comes, okay?" Ali said, a smile trying to grace her delicate features. She looked so beautiful today, thought Susan. She was beautiful every day, but today she looked especially lovely, her dark chocolate-coloured hair hanging loosely around her face. When she was working she would usually have it tied back or clipped up out of the way, but Susan loved it just how it was today, framing her face. Her tanned skin looked vibrant and healthy. There was even a small twinkle back in those blue glaciers that stared back at her.

"Okay," she acquiesced, knowing not to push. They were getting somewhere. Gradually Susan was able to introduce issues that needed to be discussed, and even if they didn't agree, she knew that Ali always heard her and would spend the time in her own head contemplating things.

~***~

Exhaustion. That was the word that best described it. Her fears about chemo had been slightly overexaggerated, which she was thankful for. It wasn't pleasant of course, but it wasn't quite as bad as she had worked herself up to believe.

There would be six cycles. Every two weeks she would go to the hospital and spend several hours with the other men and women who were all in the same boat. Some were luckier than others. They would beat it. They would go home and live their lives.

They gave her tablets for everything. Anti-sickness, steroids, and god-only-knows what. She thought she would end up rattling when she walked up the stairs. If she could walk up the stairs. She was so very tired, the first night Ali had carried her to bed. She undressed her and went to the bathroom, returning with a small basin and a cloth. She washed her. Her skin tingled and felt sore in places and she cried more from frustration than anything else, but Ali had dried her off, pulled her pyjamas on, and then taken her in her arms and held her until she fell asleep.

After several days she began to feel better. She had more energy and was able to get up and dressed. It was a beautiful day; the sun was shining high in the sky and it was warm, the kind of warm that normally Susan would enjoy, but it hurt her skin to sit outside and bask in it.

She sent Ali off to work and spent the day cooking, huge batches of food that she portioned out and placed in the freezer. She made a lasagne, chilli, and a pie. All Ali's favourites. At least they wouldn't have to worry about eating when she didn't feel up to cooking.

She then spent time clearing out her wardrobe. All the things she wouldn't need or didn't want she bagged up and would take to the charity shop. It was cathartic as well as practical. There were all these things that people held onto, and yet when push came to shove, none of it mattered. But it would matter to Ali, when the time came and she would need to throw all of her things away - it would matter. So, she was doing it now while it was still her choice to do so.

"What are you doing?" Ali asked, her long, lean frame leant at an angle by the door, her arms crossed against her chest as she watched her wife pulling shirts and tops from drawers and placing them in trash bags.

"Just organising my things," Susan answered nonchalantly.

"Why?" She took a step inside the room, and then another, until she was sitting on the edge of the bed waiting for the answer.

"Because I can?" came the reply, the back of Susan's head never turning to look at Ali as she placed a green jumper into the bag.

"I like that top." Susan knew this of course, which was why it had to go. It had to go now so that Ali didn't have to deal with it when she was gone. She couldn't bear to think of Ali sitting here like she was now, pulling out pieces of material, holding them to her face and breathing in her scent. Crying as her heart broke, deciding what to keep and what had to go. Of course, all of it had to go eventually, but for now, Susan would lessen the load.

"Really? I always thought it clashed."

"Uh huh, with your green eyes you mean?" Ali was smirking now; her wife was predictable, always had been. If there was a job to do, Susan was on it. "I'll just buy you another one, you know that, right?"

"I won't need—" She realised that Ali knew what she was doing. "I just want to be organised, you know how I am?"

Ali nodded and rose from the bed. "Well, when you're finished organising your death, please come and join me in the land of the living." She walked from the room, her heart heavy. Susan placed the sweater back into the drawer.

~***~

"I'm sorry," Susan said. She crossed the room to where Ali sat stewing in the comfortable armchair they had picked up at an old flea market. Susan had restored and recovered it, and now it was Ali's favourite chair to sit in.

She looked up at Susan, her eyes searching her face and finding only sorrow there.

"What for?"

"For being me," she answered honestly. Ali patted her lap and Susan sat, their arms wrapping around one another instinctively.

"You never have to be sorry for being you, it's why I married you. I just—" She paused, looking at the ceiling for guidance. "I just can't accept it the way you have, I need—"

"To be you?" Susan said, smiling as her wife nodded. Their foreheads met and rested together.

Chapter Six

The second bout of chemotherapy wiped Susan out. The sickness she felt from it came in waves, and although the drugs helped to alleviate it, she felt more ill than at any other time in her life. They said that next time they would give her a stronger anti-sickness drug intravenously. She could only hope that it would work, but it was of no help now.

Her body was exhausted. The smallest movement caused pain in her joints. Ali was at home and desperate to help her wife feel better. She cooked, cleaned, and kept busy while Susan slept. Their freezer had never been so full, but much to her dismay, there was nothing she could do to make things easier for Susan.

"How are you feeling? Up to eating a little soup?" Ali asked. She had only gone up to check on her, but after popping her head around the door, she had noticed Susan was awake.

"Not sure." She smiled weakly, her stomach churning at the thought. Ali walked into the room and sat beside her on the bed.

"Well, why don't I bring a small bowl up—" Susan cut her off before she could finish.

"No, can I come downstairs? I mean, would you mind?"

"Of course not, do you think you can walk or...?" she left the question in the air. If Susan needed to be carried, then she would.

Susan flipped the covers back. The energy needed just to do a simple task like that was immense.

"Take your time, there's no rush," Ali said, though every fibre of her being screamed about the lack of time; there was never enough time.

It took several minutes before Susan was upright and sitting on the edge of the bed, tears streaming down her cheeks. Wordlessly Ali scooped her up into her arms. Her physical strength would act for the both of them as she carried her out of the room.

~***~

In the few weeks since Susan's diagnosis, she had lost weight, too much weight if you asked Ali. Seven pounds to be precise, which was why Ali was worried. Susan was always thin; she couldn't afford to lose weight so drastically, but the chemo was causing several issues with her stomach.

"So, I have a half day today, and I thought that now you're feeling a little better we might go out later?" Ali asked as she brushed her wife's hair. Susan found it relaxing sitting between Ali's legs on the side of the bed.

"That would be nice, where were you thinking?"

"Well I thought maybe a short stroll around the park, and then lunch in that little café you love so much." Susan thought back to the last time they had gone out. It felt like forever since they had been anywhere. "So, I'll pick you up at around one?" Ali finished brightly, trying not to notice the amount of blonde hair on the brush. She leant forward and kissed Susan on the neck, her lips lingering there, eyes closed as she breathed in deeply and enjoyed the smell of magnolia from the body wash the blonde always used.

~***~

The park was pretty at this time of year. The flowers and trees were vibrant against the backdrop of a blue sky and green rolling grass. They strolled around the pond watching the children feed the ducks and then back again. It wasn't a long walk, but it sapped Susan of any energy. Ali placed her arm around her and supported her as they walked the short distance back to the car.

"Do you want to go home?"

"No, I'm ok, I just need to sit down for a moment." She smiled and tried to put Ali's mind at rest.

"We can go home if you want to," Ali continued, knowing Susan would try to be brave for her sake.

"No, I am quite famished now, and you promised me my favourite café," she said. Reaching out and taking Ali's hand in her own, she raised it to her lips and kissed it.

"Alright, but when you've had—"

"Enough? Yes, I will tell you. I promise."

Usually, when they ate out anywhere they would both go for the salad option, but today Ali was insistent that Susan needed 'fattening up,' and that meant burgers.

"I can't believe you're trying to make me eat burgers," Susan laughed. In all their years together, Ali had always complained about the lack of any real nutrition in junk food.

"Ah yes but, they make their own here, so it's not the same."

"Oh really, so they make healthy fries too, huh?"

Ali had to laugh; her wife was adorable when she had caught her out. "Like I said, you need fattening up. Now eat," she ordered, picking up a handful of fries and eating them. Susan did as she requested and ate as much as she could.

~***~

Before they got home, Susan was already asleep in the car. The short trip had completely exhausted her. When Ali parked the car, she stirred slightly and mumbled incoherently, making Ali smile. She carried her inside and placed her on the couch, covering her with the blanket they kept for cosy nights watching movies.

She sat opposite in the chair that was as much her as anything else in the entire house. Warm and comfortable, that was how Susan had described the chair, and therefore her wife. She tried not to think too much, but in moments like this when she was alone with her thoughts and had nothing much else to do to take her mind off of them, she would give in. She tried to force herself to imagine a world without Susan in it, but she never managed it. Her wife was everything to her; there wasn't another option.

Chapter Seven

It was a grim and wet late Wednesday afternoon when Ali came running in from the car, shaking off the jacket that she had held over her head to avoid the soaking she would have gotten from just the few yards she had to travel.

"Holy shit, it's absolutely pouring down out there," she said laughing, walking into the living room and stopping abruptly. They had a guest. "Oh, sorry."

"It's quite alright," the stranger said, smiling. She was blonde like Susan, but her hair was darker and longer than the wavy cut Susan had had recently. She sat comfortably, ankles crossed. She was attractive, Ali noted as she cast a quick eye over her. She was holding a file on her lap, manicured hands stopping it from slipping from her thighs. Coffee cups, still steaming, sat in front of them both on the coasters. The stranger reached for hers.

"Hey honey, this is Blair. She's a nurse," Susan said to Ali as though it was the most natural thing to say. A nurse, when had they discussed a nurse?

"Oh, like some kind of health visitor?" Ali asked. She tried to smile, but really, she wasn't in the mood for niceties.

"Uh—" Blair went to speak, but Susan quickly cut her off.

"Actually no, she is a nurse who I would like to help me when I find things difficult."

Ali could feel the small muscle in her jaw twitching as she tried to contain her anger. "Right. Well, I'll leave you to it then." The dark hair of her ponytail swung as she turned her back and walked out of the room.

~***~

Acceptance. One of the hardest things when dealing with cancer or any other life-threatening illness is to accept it. The diagnosis is just the beginning.

"I know you're upset with me," Susan began. "I just wanted to—"

"To find someone that can help you, yes, I get it," Ali said harshly.

"Yes."

"And I'm not good enough? I am your wife, it's my job to help you." She was shouting now; anger and hurt had eclipsed her common sense.

"What? No, of course you're good enough." She moved nearer, "But I need someone that can—"

"Can what? What can she do that I can't?"

"Do you understand what is going to happen in the coming weeks?" Susan shouted back.

"Yes. Of course I do," Ali replied, her voice shaking with emotion as she fell back against the wall.

"Do you? Really? You're prepared for the times I can't make the toilet? When I vomit all over myself because I can't keep anything down? Are you really prepared for when all I do is cry because I am in desperate pain and there is nothing you can do to ease it, when you can't touch me because my skin burns at the slightest brush of your fingers?!"

"No, no I am damn well not prepared. How can anyone be prepared for this!?" She sank to the floor, unable to hold back the tears any longer. "It's not fair," she cried as Susan dropped to her knees and held her wife in her arms as she wept. "It's just not fair."

~***~

Blair began working with Susan the following week. Her third cycle of chemo was due to start in two days, and she wanted to get into some form of routine with her new nurse and to have her settle in first. She was going to live in with them for the foreseeable future. It made more sense than having her coming and going, because Susan never knew when she might need her.

"Do you need a hand with anything?" Ali asked Blair. She had just arrived at the house and had some things in the car she needed to bring in.

"Oh sure, yes thank you." Blair followed Ali out of the front door and over to her car, unlocking the trunk. "Uh, would you grab my suitcase and I'll get—" She moved around Ali, touching her arm as she passed. "Sorry, I'll just grab this box."

"Okay." Ali picked up the case and walked off into the house. She still wasn't happy about Blair being here. She felt as though she were being replaced, that no matter how difficult things got it was her place, her job to be there to help, but she understood Susan felt differently, and that hurt.

The spare room Blair would use was down the hall from her own bedroom that she shared with Susan, separated by the bathroom. She placed the case gently on the bed and turned to leave. Blair came through the door, blocking her quick exit.

"I know that my presence here isn't something you're too keen on," Blair started to say. She noticed the look of disdain on Ali's face the moment she had set eyes on her. "I'm here to help, Ali," she continued as she moved further into the room and placed the box she was carrying down on the chest of drawers.

Ali nodded, but said nothing in reply straight away. She went to leave, but turned at the last minute.

"Have you..." She paused and sucked in a deep breath, controlled her speech before continuing. "Have you done this before?"

"Lived in as a nurse, or nursed someone with terminal cancer?" Blair asked, watching Ali close her eyes and cringe slightly at the mention of terminal cancer.

"Both."

"Yes, I nursed my mother through her cancer when I was 17. It was what made me want to become a nurse, actually. I have also nursed many other people through their last weeks. This is what I do best."

"Weeks? Susan has longer than weeks," Ali spat back.

"Of course, I didn't mean to suggest—"

"Good, because if you can't be positive about Susan's prognosis then there is no point in you being here," Ali said, closing the gap between them as she moved back into the room.

"What's going on?" Susan asked from the doorway. Looking between her wife and the nurse, she could see there was an altercation.

"Nothing," Ali said. She glanced at the woman who would now be a part of their life, and then the woman who meant everything to her.

"Ok then, shall we leave Blair to settle in?"

Ali walked towards the door and past her wife. Susan watched her walk the length of the hallway and take the stairs downwards.

"I am sorry about that, she isn't taking things very well at the moment."

"It's fine Susan, it's all part of the job." She smiled; she had dealt with much worse than Ali Jenkins. She understood Ali

Jenkins; she was no different when she was nursing her mother. She questioned everything, everyone. She was angry at the unfairness of it all, and she understood how difficult it was to keep that all inside while trying to be strong for the person actually dying.

Chapter Eight

Ali dropped Susan off at the hospital. She had wanted to stay with her for her treatment, but Susan had insisted that it wasn't necessary and that she would be fine; she would talk to Mary and Jean, who were on the same cycle as she was.

So, Ali went home, having promised to try and spend some time relaxing before she picked her up again at three o'clock. Relaxing had become something that was easier said than done recently. There was so much to do, so much to talk about. Relaxing by herself was not on her list of things to do.

Arriving back at the house, Ali found herself sitting outside in the car, her thoughts wandered back and forth, from the first time she had met Susan to ten minutes ago when she had kissed her goodbye.

She didn't notice the shadow of someone approaching. Blair had seen the car pull up and had watched as Ali sat still in the car. When she still hadn't come in after ten minutes, she made the decision to go out and check on her. The nurse found her employer's wife with her eyes closed and her cheeks wet. She tapped gently on the window and waved apologetically when Ali jumped in her seat.

Ali wiped her cheeks with the back of her hands and then switched off the engine before climbing out of the car.

"Sorry, I wasn't—".

"Its fine, I uh—"

"You don't need to explain, Ali. I get it." Blair spoke gently, her words sincere. Ali swallowed the lump that had been constricting her throat more often than not lately.

"Yeah, if you'll excuse me?" she replied, anxious to get inside now.

~***~

Blair sat quietly in the kitchen. A cup of coffee was within reach on the countertop in front of her, and her magazine was opened to the page she was reading last. She could hear Ali descending the stairs, her footsteps heavy and slow as she allowed herself to wallow a little while Susan was out of the picture. It would do her good, thought Blair, she needed to wallow and flounder and fall apart when she could. It was the only way she was going to get through this.

She sat quietly while Ali wandered the kitchen behind her, pouring boiling water into a mug and adding milk; the soft tinkle of the spoon hitting the sides as she stirred. Blair could feel the eyes on her, but she remained quiet, sipping her coffee and reading her article.

She had learnt a long time ago that you had to allow people their space; they had to come to you, because any other way would only ever be taken as interference. If it took Ali a week or a month to come around to the fact that she was only here to help, then she would deal with the attitude, because she understood it. She had been Ali.

So far Ali had not willingly allowed Blair to take on any aspect of Susan's care, which was fine because the last couple of days Susan didn't particularly need her to help with her care. Today, though, would be different. Today was the third cycle of chemotherapy, and from what Susan had explained, they were slowly taking their toll on her, exhaustion mainly but also a terrible sickness and pain; her muscles ached. Her hair loss was also becoming more notable.

"She's not going to die." Ali's voice was low. A sadness saturated her, but she was firm. "Not yet. I mean, I know she is—" And then her voice cracked. "I know she is going to, but—"

Blair turned in her seat to face the desperate woman who stood there, her eyes glistening with unshed tears, a defiance set in her jawline. One hand was tucked in her jeans pocket, the other holding the hot mug of coffee.

"No, not yet."

"But soon?" Ali asked, the tears falling freely. Blair nodded.

"In my experience..." she began, but checked herself and asked, "Do you want to know?" Ali nodded but didn't look at her, the tiled flooring holding her attention. "In my experience, most people with stage four breast cancer that has spread to the brain usually have between three and twelve months." She saw the pain flash across Ali's face. "But that doesn't mean it will be the same for Susan."

"I need—" Ali began, her throat tightening. "I need you to be honest with me. I might not take it well. I might be a complete asshole, but I need to hear it."

"Alright, I can do that."

"I don't want her to know about, about today or any other time I get upset."

"Ali, I am not here to be a go-between or to tattle tale on either of you. My job is to make sure that Susan is comfortable, to make sure she has the right—" she needed to be careful with how she worded things. "The right care for her treatments. It's your job to provide her with the emotional care, Ali. It's you she will want to spend her time with."

Ali nodded and moved to sit at the breakfast bar next to Blair.

"Ya know it's in my interests to keep her healthy for as long as possible."

Ali squinted her gaze at her, unsure what she meant.

"Otherwise I don't get paid." She smiled and for the first time, Ali returned it.

~***~

Collecting Susan from the hospital later, Ali made sure to plaster a smile on her face and greet her wife with a cheerful 'hey'.

Her smile soon turned to a frown as she noticed the red-rimmed eyes that returned her smile. They were sitting in the room where Susan received her treatment. It was a nice room, brightly decorated with comfortable chairs for long hours of sitting in; it smelt clean. Everyone else had left for the day, other than a few nurses and clinicians who were tidying and cleaning.

"You ok?" Ali asked, a stupid question but the best she could come up with. She took a seat on the chair next to her. Susan shook her head and began to sob. Her instant reaction was to reach out and wrap her arms around the blonde, pull her close and embrace her. However, the whimper of pain that escaped her wife's lips was enough to pull her back instantly. She hated this, hated not being able to comfort her in the way they were so used to doing.

"Susan, baby, please. What's wrong? Is it the chemo?"

"No, yes, I mean yes the chemo is affecting me, my skin hurts, I'm just so tired but—" She looked at Ali with such sorrow. "Jean, the lady who I have been talking with each cycle?" Ali nodded, Jean and Mary were the names Susan mentioned after each session. "Jean, she didn't come in today."

"Ok." Ali wasn't sure why this was so upsetting, but she went along with Susan anyway.

"She didn't come in because—" Susan sobbed once more. Ali reached out and hooked their pinkie fingers together, the need to touch her all too important. "She passed away last night and I guess, I suppose it just brought it home to me that one day, that's going to be me."

"Oh sweetheart, I'm so sorry."

"I know I shouldn't be so surprised, but—" The words died off and instead she added, "Let's go home, huh?" She sighed, wiping her eyes once again with the tissue Ali had passed across from the box by the side of them. "I think I'll need a wheelchair, my love." Her smile was weak and weary.

"Okay, I'll be right back." She stood, smiling tightly as she fought to hold it all in. With every step she walked, a tear slid slowly down her cheek. It hadn't gone unnoticed that one day there would be somebody else sitting in a chair just like Susan, crying because her friend didn't make it through the night. She concentrated on every step, aware that at any point she might stumble and fall; break apart, and then what? So she sucked in a breath and held her head high and carried on, because the very least Susan deserved was for Ali to hold it together.

Chapter Nine

For Blair, it was a busy few days. Her nursing skills were pushed to their limits with Susan in constant pain. Several times she had had to change her, the nausea coming in waves that gave no warning. She would spend hours curled up into a ball in her bed, weeping silently. It broke Blair's heart when any of her clients were suffering like this, and she only hoped she could help Susan to get through it and save Ali from witnessing the discomfort her wife was in.

With her painkillers finally starting to take hold on the third day, Ali was able to embrace her at last, and it was evident that both of them needed it.

"Ya know, I was thinking maybe some fresh air might do you good," Ali stated, as she spooned her in bed that morning. The room was stale, and the scent of vomit and other bodily functions clung to the air. It didn't bother Ali, she would tolerate anything if it meant her wife was comfortable, but she knew it would bother Susan.

"I would like that; would you help me get dressed?"

"Of course, any excuse to have me checking you out, right?" Ali joked. Susan felt Ali's smile against her back where she rested her warm lips. She kissed her bare shoulder before rising from the bed. "Shower or bath?"

"Bath please, the water power is a little harsh at the moment for a shower." Susan smiled but closed her eyes and rested a little longer. Everything was such hard work.

"Ok, be right back. Don't go anywhere." Ali continued with her light-hearted chatter.

"I won't, nowhere else I'd rather be." The smile lingered on her lips, until Ali left the room and she could breathe deeply until the nausea passed.

~***~

The water was warm, barely hot enough had Ali been having the bath, but for Susan it was perfect. Too much heat was painful for her. Ali slipped back into the bedroom and gently touched her arm. Her eyes opened and she grinned lazily up at the woman she loved so much.

"Hi," Ali whispered.

"Hello again."

"Remember me?"

"Yes, I believe you're my nurse for this morning, Ali wasn't it?" she chuckled, glad they could still have these moments of humour between each other.

"That's right, and that means you have to let me undress you and touch you inappropriately—" She laughed, helping her wife to sit up. "Oh, no that's not right, is it? I have to undress you and put you in the bath." She began undoing the buttons on her sleep top, trying to keep her face from registering the shock she always felt when she saw how ravaged her wife's beautiful body had become. She kissed her lightly on the lips, focusing on the positive. They still had time.

"Uh huh, though I wouldn't tell your boss if you were to touch me." She winked, fully aware just how ravaged she looked but not willing to mention it and break the spell. "You're hot."

"Naughty, I'll have to warn the other staff of your wicked ways," she replied, sliding her pyjama bottoms down her once-muscular thighs, her fingers lightly tracing a path as they followed the cotton material. It had shocked Ali how quickly her body had wasted away.

Ali lifted Susan's naked form up into the air, holding her against herself and taking joy in the feel of her thin arms wrapping around her neck as they walked the short distance to the waiting bath. Lowering her gently into the water, she held on until the very last minute when she was sure she was okay and then quickly stripped off her own clothes and climbed in behind her.

"Is this a new form of nursing I haven't been told about?" Susan teased as Ali soaked a sponge and added some body wash, her gentle hands sponging the skin in front of her before tugging gently on her to lie back and relax, letting Ali support her completely.

"Well, I have suggested it, but so far nobody seems as keen. I am not sure why?"

"Good thing I get you then and not the other one. Although I think Blair might enjoy a bath with you."

Ali laughed and soaked the sponge again, washing the suds away. Susan was just skin and bones at the moment, another symptom of the chemo. Who wanted to eat when everything just came back up anyway? According to Blair, her weight loss wasn't actually as bad as Ali feared, and when the chemotherapy was finished then her appetite would return and she would gain a little of her lost weight back. They were feeding her a lot of supplements to make sure she had all the right things to help her fight.

"I highly doubt the nurse has time to consider bathing with me!" Ali snorted.

She poured a little shampoo into her hands and began to wash her wife's hair. When she felt the small clumps come away she couldn't stop the flow of tears, but silently she continued, rinsing and conditioning, rinsing once more, leaving the pile of lost hair on the edge of the bath.

"I was thinking maybe I should just shave it all off," Susan said, clearly aware that her hair was beginning to fall out now.

"Uh huh," Ali answered, her throat constricting and stopping her from making any further comment.

"I've never had short hair before." The conversation was so simple, a matter of fact being discussed as though it was nothing to worry about, and yet Ali couldn't imagine having to cut off her own hair.

"I think whatever length your hair is, you will still be beautiful." She pushed her hands through the space under Susan's arms and hugged her, arms crossing her chest, her hands resting on her shoulders. Susan could feel the warmth of breath on her neck and felt calmness flood through her.

"I think you're biased, but I'll accept the compliment." She raised her own hands, the water dripping from them as she placed them on top of Ali's. "I love it when you hold me like this."

"Mm, I love it when I hold you like this too. But, this water is getting too cold, and you need to dry off and get dressed before you catch—" She was about to say 'your death of cold.'

"You can say it, Ali, I'm not that sensitive yet." She chuckled and squeezed her fingers. She felt her lover rest her forehead against her.

"I love you," Ali whispered.

"And I love you. You are my everything Ali Jenkins, always have been."

~***~

It was warm outside, but Susan looked as though she were on a snow-capped mountain with the number of blankets she had wrapped around her. She felt the cold a lot more lately than she had ever done. Ali thought she looked particularly adorable in the bobble hat she was wearing. She flicked her phone open and took a quick selfie of them snuggling together on the deck in the hammock-style seat they had bought a few years ago. It was the same seat they had made love on under the stars when Ali had finally given in and read the instructions on how to put it all together.

From the window, Blair watched them. Over the years she had witnessed many a couple together in their last months, weeks, and days. She had seen husbands become workaholics because they couldn't deal with it. She watched as wives fussed and pestered husbands until it drove them nuts. She had seen families fall apart, grow closer, change beyond recognition, but watching Ali and Susan, she realised she had never witnessed a couple just be in love with each other.

Susan lay cradled between Ali's strong thighs, Ali's left arm wrapped securely around Susan's waist, with Susan's hand tucked warmly underneath. Their right hands were linked with tangled fingers. Her head rested perfectly against Ali's shoulder, and they were laughing. A lot of couples struggled to find laughter, struggled to find any positive from the diagnosis. It was good to see, and she hoped they had as much time as possible to keep on enjoying each other.

Chapter Ten

"I want you to do it," Susan said as Ali was brushing her teeth and Blair was organising the bedclothes. Susan stood in the doorway in her blue silk dressing gown, the one Ali had bought for her the previous Christmas. Her cheeks were much rosier today, Ali had noted. She was feeling much better in herself, up and about without too much fuss, and Ali was buoyed by it.

"Why me? I have never cut hair before," Ali replied after spitting out the toothpaste froth that had accumulated around her teeth.

"I don't think hairdressing is a skill you need to be fair Ali, just a steady hand with the razor." Susan caught Blair looking on at the conversation and they both shared a small giggle.

"A razor?" came the high-pitched exclamation from the bathroom. Blair snorted and Susan giggled some more.

"Yes sweetheart, just chop all the long pieces off with some scissors and then shave the rest of it off with a razor, I think it would be quite simple really."

"I think you are mistaking me for someone that isn't aware that you two are laughing at me?" she said, walking into the bedroom and catching them both stifling their laughter. "I knew it," she said seriously, but followed up the statement with a sexy smirk, the same sexy smirk that had Susan's heart aflutter the day they went on their first official date.

"So, you'll do it then?" Susan asked, batting her eyelashes overdramatically.

"Like I could deny you anything!" Ali said, pulling her into a hug and kissing her gently. "When?"

"Now?"

"Now?" The high-pitched squeal came again, causing Blair and Susan to once more burst into laughter. "Dear lord, what did I do to deserve this," Ali said with mock horror, throwing her hands in the air and walking back into the bathroom.

Blair had gone back to her own room by the time Ali returned with the tools she would need. She had a pair of scissors and a small bowl of warm water with the razor and some soap, a towel draped over her left arm.

"You sure you want to do this right now?" she asked as she placed each item down firmly on the dresser.

"Yes, I have my head around the idea and I am ready to do it, are you?"

"I haven't been ready for any of this, but I am doing it anyway," Ali said honestly. She found everything about this situation difficult, but she would get a grip on it for Susan's sake.

"I can ask Blair if you would prefer."

"No, this is my job," she said, remembering back to the talk she and Blair had shared. It was her job to be there for Susan emotionally, and she wanted that job; it was a job she held dear, and she wouldn't fail.

Susan sat carefully on the stool in front of the dresser while Ali placed everything within easy reach. She placed the towel around her neck and then gently brushed her hair through. It was coming away quite easily now, so it probably was the right time to do this, if there ever could be a right time to shave your head. They shared a look through the mirror: Ali's a question, and Susan's the answer. And so, Ali began to cut the hair. She started on the back and placed each section lovingly in a small box that Susan hadn't seen her bring in. It didn't take very long. Susan kept her eyes closed the entire time. She listened as the shaving soap was squeezed from the aerosol can into Ali's palm and felt the coolness as it touched her scalp, Ali's gentle fingers tenderly rubbing it into the remaining hair. She heard her wash her fingers in the bowl and the soft swish of the towel as she dried them, and then she heard her speak.

"Ready?"

She replied with a nod, a single tear dripping slowly down her right cheek. She heard Ali take a deep breath and exhale slowly, then a small kiss on the base of her neck, and then she felt the blade as it dragged across her scalp from the centre of her forehead to the nape of her neck. Over and over the blade moved, deftly held by her wife's loving hand.

When she felt no further movement, she opened her eyes. She expected to be shocked, to burst into tears and not like it at all, but to her surprise, she wasn't that upset at all.

"You look like a pixie," Ali said, watching for her reaction. Her ears stood out more without hair to balance them.

"I do." She laughed and turned her head one way, then the other, her fingers gently touching the bare scalp. "I guess it will look better when it grows back a little bit."

"I guess you could always wear a—"

"Do not say wig!" Susan snorted. "I am not going to. I'll wear hats or scarves if I decide I don't like it."

~***~

Thirty minutes later and Susan was snoring lightly. She lay comfortably on her back supported by several pillows, but the position caused her to snore; always had done. Her newly shorn head stood out starkly against the backdrop of ice white pillows.

Ali lay on her side of the bed in the dark, her thoughts all over the place as she tried to once more adjust to another emotionally draining day, her hand resting lovingly on Susan's arm. It was no use; she couldn't sleep, and so she quietly climbed from their bed and left the room.

She found herself standing outside Blair's bedroom door, contemplating whether she was awake or not. The lights in the house were off and it was dark in the hallway, but she could see the gentle light of a lamp emitting from under the door.

She knocked lightly and waited, her arms wrapped around her tightly as she rocked back and forth on the balls of her feet. She was about to turn and walk back to her own room when the door opened slowly.

"Hey, is she ok?" Blair asked quietly. Ali nodded but continued to stare at the floor, biting her lower lip. "Are you ok?" Blair said just as quietly, reaching out to touch Ali on her arm. This time Ali shook her head slowly. Her chin wobbled, and as she finally raised her eyes upwards, Blair witnessed the cascade of tears as they fell freely down her cheeks. "Oh Ali, come here." She reached for her, and for the first time, Ali fell into her waiting arms and allowed Blair to soothe her.

~***~

When Susan appeared for breakfast the following morning, she found both Blair and Ali sitting together at the breakfast bar wearing sunglasses. As she approached, they both raised their hands to their eyes and grimaced.

"Oh my god!" cried Ali. "Please, the glare from your bald head is blinding me!"

Blair joined in the fun. "I can't see!"

"Oh, very funny, the both of you." Susan chuckled and hit them both with a dish towel as she flicked out a wrist. "Where's my breakfast, I am famished."

Blair and Ali were still laughing, and it pleased Susan to see Ali finally accepting Blair and what she was there for. They were getting along. She hoped in Blair that Ali would find a friend, an ally in the months ahead. Something had changed between them, she could tell that much; no longer did Ali grimace or mutter under her breath when she thought no one could hear.

"Oh, milady would like breakfast? Well come right this way," Ali said, bowing theatrically and then leading the way to the dining room. The table was set for two, all their best plates and cutlery shined to perfection. A vase of fresh flowers cut from the garden sat centre stage. There were glasses of freshly squeezed orange juice, a jug of iced water, a plate piled high with pancakes, jars of maple syrup and honey, a bowl of fruit salad, and another plate with croissants.

"Oh Ali, this is beautiful."

"Well, I thought you deserved a treat," she said, holding the chair out in order for her to sit. "Would you like some coffee?" she asked, raising the pot and pouring a small cup for herself and then, when Susan agreed, pouring a second cup.

The sunlight from the window lit up Susan's face as they sat eating in a comfortable silence. Occasionally Susan would stroke

Ali's cheek or Ali would hold her hand, the need to touch and caress one another as strong now as it ever was.

"Have you got any plans for today?" Susan asked as they finished their meal. Ali shook her head.

"Nope, just to spend it with you. What would you like to do?"

"Well, would you mind doing something we've never done before?" Her smile lit up her face even more than the sunlight.

"You're beautiful," Ali said, suddenly taken with the need to tell her.

"Thank you for saying that." She blushed a little, and her smile turned shy as she looked at her plate. Ali put her finger under her chin and raised her face up to look at her.

"I mean it, you have always been beautiful, and that hasn't changed." She let her palm slide effortlessly to cup Susan's cheek as she leaned into it.

"I have loved you since we were 15 years old." Now it was Ali's turn to blush. "When I first saw you on the school bus and you smiled at me as I passed by, I thought to myself that I was going to find a way to talk to you."

"And you did." Ali chuckled at the memory.

"Yes, although literally falling at your feet hadn't been the original plan," Susan remembered fondly.

"No, but it worked. I picked you up and said—"

"'Hey, are you ok?' And then you looked at me with those big blue eyes, and I was lost in them. I never understood then what it meant, to love another woman, to me you were just beautiful." Her arms slid more tightly around Ali's neck as she leaned forward in her chair.

"I am so grateful that we met so young, that we have had all these years to spend getting to know each other, and that I got to fall in love with you," Ali continued, her own arms tightening around her wife's waist.

"When you started dating Sandra? Oh, I hated her." Susan grinned at the memory.

"Well, she was pretty annoying."

"Yes, she was, and more annoying was that she had you. For years!" She moved closer, shifted in her seat and kissed Ali gently on the lips. "I wanted so badly to tell you how I felt. I used to lie awake thinking up ways to tell you."

"I wish I had known. I loved you from the moment you fell at my feet. I wanted to scoop you up and kiss you all better, but I didn't understand why. And then later when I fully understood why, you were dating David. So there it was, my first crush on a straight friend."

"Oh God, David. Bless his heart, he was so sweet to me."

Ali moved her chair back and patted her lap for Susan to sit. She kissed her, a long, slow, languid kiss that said so much more than just 'I love you'.

"We've been together for over twelve years, married for eight." Susan watched Ali nod and smile. "And I would love you for eternity if I could." They kissed again; it was shorter this time but filled with as much meaning as the last. She studied her face, her eyes locked firmly with her wife's as she uttered the next sentence. "I want you to let someone else love you."

"Susan, don't—" She felt a soft finger touch her lips as Susan shushed her.

"I want you to let someone else in, when I am gone, when the time is right. You have forty or more years left of life, if you are lucky, and—"

"Nobody can replace you Susan, nobody," she said vehemently.

"I don't want them to replace me, baby, you'll always be mine and I'll always be yours, but there is room in this heart of yours for someone else. Let someone else into your heart, Ali."

The silence in the room was echoed only by the beating of two hearts. Two hearts aching for one another.

"You didn't tell me what you want to do today," Ali said, deciding that a change of subject would be the best course to take. Avoidance. Susan smiled, acknowledging that she had pushed as far as she could for today.

"I want to ride a horse."

Chapter Eleven

Bucket list. Something you compile, a list of things you've yet to do and want to try before you die.

And apparently Susan had one. After the horse riding adventure had been such a success, Susan had begun to think of all the simple things she had yet to do and wanted to achieve, as well as all the things she loved doing and wanted to do one last time.

"Ok, seriously?" Ali said as she read through the list of things Susan had written in her little notebook. She was sitting up in bed, her back against the pillows while Susan was washing up and removing her make-up. "I am pretty sure we have done some of these already," she called out, a blush deepening on her cheeks. "Did you say Blair had read this list?"

"Yes, she helped me write it," Susan said, poking her head around the door as she wiped her face with a cotton pad. "What are you complaining about?"

"Well, I am not complaining, I'm just surprised is all."

"About?" She knew exactly which parts of her wish list would have surprised her wife, but she enjoyed teasing her anyway.

"Oh come on, Susan. You know which parts! The parts where you want to try all these new positions. The Pleasure Perch?

Really? What is that? And how do you even know about it and I don't?"

Susan waltzed into the room in her dressing gown that hung slightly open, revealing a little and leaving a lot more to the imagination.

"Blair and I were talking and she mentioned the lesbian Kama Sutra and so—"

"Hang on, you and Blair were talking about sex?" Ali asked, her eyes never leaving her wife as she watched her move about the room. "Lesbian sex?"

"Yes, well she mentioned an old girlfriend had suggested spicing up—"

"Wait." Ali held a palm in the air. "Back up. Her girlfriend?"

"Yes, honestly Ali, I figured you at least would be the one of us to have her inner gaydar working." She smiled sweetly as she stood at the side of the bed and untied her robe, letting it fall to the floor behind her. Her cotton PJs had been replaced by a sexy black negligee. It hung more loosely on her than it used to, but for Ali, she was still the beautiful, sexy woman she always had been, if not more so now, her unwavering bravery a surprising turn-on.

"Well, excuse me for not perving on the nurse more appropriately," she said, distracted now.

"So, do you want me to show you what the Pleasure Perch is?" She climbed seductively up onto the bed and crawled across to

Ali's side, then kissed her shoulder, making her way gently up her neck to her earlobe and then across to her mouth, where she hovered so close she could feel their breath mingle. "I demand to try every single one of those positions." Their lips touched, the briefest of caresses. "And I want to start with some 'lip service.'"

"Then I suggest you start explaining what the hell that is before all your energy gets zapped from me kissing you." Ali placed her hand behind Susan's head, the sharp stubble tickling her palm as she pulled her mouth down to meet her own.

Susan taught Ali all about the Kama Sutra. She surprised Ali with just how explicit she could be. They had never had any trouble communicating in the bedroom before, but now, there was no opportunity at all for a miscommunication. Susan told her exactly what she wanted, and she enjoyed every second of giving it to her.

Attention. Susan now had Ali's, all of it, unwavering and decisive. Their lovemaking had changed a lot over the last few weeks. As a couple, they had always made the effort to keep their relationship fresh and exciting, and that wasn't going to change as far as either of them was concerned. Making love was a huge part of their expression of emotion towards one another. Of course, the diagnosis and the treatments would make it a little difficult at times, downright awkward at others, but there would be no surrender until time ran out.

~***~

Some mornings are made for lying in bed, and this was one of them. Blair wasn't too surprised when nobody joined her for breakfast. Her discussion with Susan a few days earlier had given her the heads up that as soon as she felt up to it physically, she was going to enjoy a night of love with Ali, though she hadn't told Ali that was her plan. She was so frustrated with having to plan everything around her illness; she wanted some spontaneity for them both. One night where they could just be themselves.

Blair had helped her to prepare by making sure she ate at the right time and took a nap and a bath while Ali was working. It took a lot of preparation to make sure her energy levels were at the top of her game. Blair helped her pick out the outfit that fit best and then retired to her room so they had the privacy of their home.

As she finished her second cup of coffee, the sound of movement on the stairs caught her ear. The sight of Ali brightly skipping down the steps made her smile. The grin on Ali's face was a lovely enough sight to brighten anyone's day.

"Good morning," Blair said, watching as Ali entered the room and grabbed a mug from the draining board.

"Hey," she replied with another smile. "You want another cup?"

"No, thank you. Had two already, any more and I will be bouncing off the walls," she said, holding her mug in the air as evidence.

Ali poured the dark, hot liquid into her mug, added some milk, and sat down on the bar stool next to Blair. She then slumped dramatically onto her arms and groaned.

"Busy night?" Blair asked, suppressing a giggle.

"Uh huh, someone got it into their head to tick off a few things on their bucket list," she said, raising her head and an eyebrow. "Apparently someone else gave her a few pointers." She smirked.

"Oh, well uh—" Blair stuttered a little before rallying. "Hang on, all of them?"

"All of them!" Ali assured her. They both burst into laughter and sat together considering that little piece of information.

"So, I guess she is wiped out now, huh?" Blair asked, nodding knowingly.

"Yeah, she said to wake her up for lunch." Another chuckle. "But the plus side is, she is in a good mood."

Both women fell about laughing once more before setting about cleaning up the mess they had made. It was a pleasant time for Ali. Now that she was no longer so against having Blair here, she found she liked the woman. They had a lot in common and a shared sense of humour. It made life a lot easier, she had to admit. Coming home from work the first few days had been daunting. She had spent all day worrying that Susan would be struggling, but with Blair, she was keeping her independence. Blair never did things for her; she just assisted her to be able to do it for herself. But on those occasions when she really couldn't manage, then Blair would deal with things; no fuss, no judgement, just a professional and caring manner that kept Susan positive and, for the most part, smiling.

~***~

"I can keep her company if there is anything you want to go and do," Blair said to Ali later in the day. Susan had woken and come downstairs for a light lunch, insisting on staying put on the couch. They were watching a movie, but she fell asleep once more, her head lying comfortably in Ali's lap. Blair covered her with the blanket and they continued to watch the movie.

"No, thank you. I am happy right here where I am meant to be," she answered, her gaze on her wife's sleeping face the picture of adoration.

"You really love each other, don't you?" Blair stated; it was a fact she couldn't deny. Ali caught her gaze and held it firm.

"Yes, she's my world. I don't—" She fought to contain the pools of tears that filled her eyes. "I am struggling with trying to imagine a life without her in it."

"I felt something similar when my mother passed. I was seventeen and knew nothing of the world around me," Blair acknowledged.

"No offense but, it isn't the same. Our parents are supposed to die before we do, our partners are not supposed to die before they hit 35," she answered angrily before pushing her hand through her hair and apologising. "I'm sorry, that was uncalled for."

"It's ok," Blair said. "You did warn me you might be an asshole," she continued, raising a comical brow.

Ali couldn't help but smile, the joke lightening the mood instantly and making it easier to keep talking. She was good at this, Ali thought, Blair was really good at this. Maybe she wasn't here to just help Susan; she was helping Ali too.

Chapter Twelve

Life for the Jenkins was an up and down affair. With Susan halfway through her chemotherapy and about to undertake the fourth cycle, they would have just over a week of life being relatively normal, with enough energy and enthusiasm to take on most things, ticking off items on the list and spending time together. But for four or five days life would be difficult. Susan would struggle with the effects of the chemo, and Ali would struggle with not being able to take it all away from her. Blair was there to pick up the slack and keep everything running smoothly. She dealt with the things that Susan was adamant she did not want Ali to witness; embarrassing and intimate things.

In their life together, of course, Ali had seen Susan at her worst. She had held her hair when she had been unwell, she had bathed her and cooked for her, all the things a partner does over the course of a marriage, and that was all fine. Susan could accept that because none of those things were fresh memories.

She had two things on her mind with regard to Ali:

1. Leave her with only good memories of her.

2. Leave her open to finding love again.

~***~

On days like these, Ali always found a way to try and be home a little earlier. She took time off on the days when Susan felt better so they could enjoy time together doing things that required daylight and sunshine.

She spent her afternoons and evenings mainly with Blair. They would share a meal together quite often, and Blair would fill her in on all of the day's events, including the things she found uncomfortable to hear, but had insisted she wanted to know about.

"She had a bad day today." Blair spoke with a gentleness she knew Ali would appreciate. "The stomach issues she has been dealing with were the worst so far." She didn't tell her about the need to use an adult diaper, something Susan really didn't want to share. She was adamant that she didn't want Ali to have to change her.

"Has she eaten anything?"

"Only the supplement drinks. Don't worry though, as unpleasant as it is for her to deal with, it is all quite usual for a lot of people. They have given her a different anti-emetic, which has really helped with her nausea."

"Well, at least there is one positive. Is she ok, in herself?"

"Yeah, she is pretty upbeat considering she feels like shit and can't move without the need to sleep for an hour." Her smile was warm and understanding. "But she is looking forward to seeing you."

"I'll head on up then."

~***~

She pushed the door open and entered the darkened room. The window was open a little to allow some fresh air into the stale environment. It had been two days since Susan's last chemo treatment.

Susan stirred and mumbled something incoherent.

"Hey baby, I heard someone was waiting for me to come up and say hi," Ali whispered. Taking a seat on the edge of the bed, she bent her head lower and kissed her wife's forehead.

"Hey," she answered, her eyes still closed. "What time is it?" She knew Ali was sneaking home earlier and earlier. The only days she seemed to be at the office for the entire day were the ones when Susan's friends or family came to visit.

"No idea. I was in too much of a hurry to come up here and kiss the beautiful woman in my bed." She nuzzled her nose against her cheek and kissed her once again.

"You are full of it." Susan chuckled, her eyes slowly opening. They flickered back and forth as she strained to clear her sleepy vision.

"Now now, you know I'm right. How are you feeling?"

"Hmm, a bit better I think." She slowly raised her hand to rub her sleepy eyes. Ali stood to get her some water.

"Ali?" she called urgently. "Ali?"

"I'm here, what's up?" She held the glass in front of her for Susan to take, but she didn't move.

"Ali, I can't see. I can't see anything." She sounded panicked, and Ali felt a surge of terror.

"Ok, it's probably just a side effect of the new drug." She walked to the door and called for Blair, the nurse arriving moments later.

"Blair, Susan says she can't see," Ali explained, her voice unsteady and nervous. She was pacing, her hands in her hair.

"Ok, let's all stay calm," Blair said. She walked up to the side of the bed and bent down to rest on her knees. She took Susan's hand in her own and used her other hand to guide her face around to look at her. "Tell me exactly what you can see."

"Just shadows, everything is blurred. I can see you're in front of me, but I can't make out your face," she answered, her voice now as calm and quiet as Blair's had been.

"Ok, I am going to shine a light on you. Tell me if you notice a change." Blair pulled a small yellow-coloured medical flashlight from her pocket and swung it back and forth in front of her face, but not directly into her eyes.

"Yes, I can see a brightness." She smiled.

"Ok, I think we need to get you checked out by the hospital." She could feel the tension in Ali before she even looked at her. "Ali, would you find some clothes for Susan to wear while I get her bathed and ready?" The instructions immediately gave Ali something to focus on, and she set about her task eagerly. "And when you are done, would you put together a small light lunch that we can take with us in case Susan gets hungry?"

Susan used all of her strength to get out of bed, and with Blair's help, they made it to the bathroom. Once the door was closed she said, "I don't think I am going to want to eat."

"I know, but she will, and she needs something to keep her busy right now," Blair answered, undressing her and washing her down.

"I knew there was a reason I liked you." Susan chuckled. "Do you think this is serious?"

"It could be a sign that the tumour in your brain is affecting your sight, yes." She watched Susan nod. Understanding.

"And that would mean the chemo isn't working, wouldn't it?" she continued, probing for answers.

"That's always been a possibility," Blair answered honestly.

Chapter Thirteen

The doctor's office hadn't changed; it still contained the same stark white walls and bright airy space that it had the last time Susan was there, only this time she couldn't see it. She sat with Ali to her right and Blair to her left as the doctor began to explain the results of the scans and tests.

"Basically, there are a few options we have. Number one would be to operate immediately and try to remove as much of the tumour as we can and hope that it alleviates the problem. Two would be to try a different round of chemotherapy once you have finished this one, although we would have to wait a while between them in order to give your body a little time to gain its strength back, or radiation therapy."

"And option three?" Ali asked, hopeful of some new miracle drug that might be on offer.

"Option three would be to—" The doctor sat back in her chair and licked her bottom lip before finishing. "Would be to withdraw all treatments and allow nature to take its course."

Ali felt the rush of air leave her body. The miracle wouldn't be happening, and they were now discussing the idea of Susan giving up.

"You mean let her die?" Ali was livid. "That's not an option," she said, shaking her head furiously. Her mind swept away all conscious thought. As the conversation continued around her, she sank further into her seat.

"...how long do I have if..."

"...we decided to go down that road, what would be the risk?"

"...all a lot to take in right now, and you should go home and discuss it before you reach a decision."

Ali heard bits and pieces of the conversation, her brain having difficulty in keeping up with everything that was said. She hated these appointments.

~***~

They had dinner in relative silence before retiring to their room, the events of the day taking their toll on all of them. Susan's eyesight would come and go. Sometimes it would be complete blindness and other times she would just suffer a blur to one eye. There was no rhyme or reason to it, and at the moment she could see Ali pretty well.

She could tell Ali was struggling. She didn't need to be able to see to know that; she could feel it. It was tangible.

"Are you ready to talk about it?" Susan asked Ali, knowing full well she knew what she was meant.

"Nope," Ali said instantly, moving around the room as she undressed and threw all their dirty clothes into the wash basket. She walked naked to the bathroom, and Susan sighed deeply before she made herself comfortable against the upright pillows.

"Alison Jane Jenkins, you come out of there right now and sit with me," Susan demanded. It took a minute, but Ali walked back out of the bathroom and slowly over to the bed, her head hanging low, lips pursed.

"I get it, I know you want to bury your head in the sand and pretend none of this is happening, but you can't," Susan said, taking her wife's hands in her own. She moved to kneel on the bed next to where Ali sat. "You have to listen at the very least because I need to say things that you need to hear."

Ali looked at her now, frightened about the things Susan wanted to say. Her blue eyes were cloudy and haunted as they stared at the green ones looking back at her.

"I am dying," she sighed. Ali dropped her head once more. "No, you don't get to look away from me. I need you."

"I'm here," Ali mumbled. Susan cupped her cheek and stroked her thumb lovingly across her soft skin.

"I don't want to spend what is left of my life feeling like this." She had to take a breath. The sight of her wife's silent tears finally falling caused the lump in her throat to expand. "I have accepted that I am going to die and—" Ali tried to speak, but she stopped her. "No, let me finish," she said, waiting for Ali to wipe her eyes.

The strong jawline she loved so much tensed and twitched as Ali held herself quiet. "If you want me to have this operation I will do it, if you want me to continue with more chemo then I will do it but, you need to understand that none of it will change the outcome. My cancer is spreading and the chemo isn't working." Ali slumped against her, her shoulders shaking as the uncontrollable sobs wracked her body. Unable to hold it in any longer, she cried out like a wounded animal. Blair entered the room urgently thinking that Susan needed her, but backed out quietly once Susan indicated she was fine, and she saw that it was Ali who had cried out in pain.

When they were alone again she pulled her wife into her side and let them both fall back onto the bed, where she held her and rocked her until the sobs lessened, until neither of them was able to fight sleep any longer.

~***~

The doctor explained that the radiation therapy would consist of one treatment a day for a period of two weeks. They would target the tumour, and if things worked well, then hopefully they would look at a second round of chemotherapy. If it didn't, then Susan wanted to go to option three.

They had discussed the options at length. Ali had tried every argument she had, but in the end, she had to agree with Susan that quality time together would be better than time spent unwell. They both fully understood that if Susan chose to stop her treatments then the likelihood was that three months would be the estimated time they would have.

"We can begin on Monday if that's okay with you, Susan? Do you have any further questions?" Dr Meyer asked, looking at both Susan and Ali.

"No, thank you, I believe Blair has given me the rundown on what to expect, which is pretty much exactly what I have been dealing with already so, the sooner we get this over with the better," Susan explained. "Thank you for everything, Doctor Meyer. I think my wife and I would like to enjoy the weekend together while we still can." There was an edge to Susan's voice. If truth be told, she didn't really want to do this. She was doing it for Ali, because Ali needed her to fight. But Susan had accepted her fate and was okay with it; she had come to realise that life didn't always work out how you planned it to. You didn't always get to finish what you started.

Blair caught the wince on Ali's features the moment Susan finished her sentence. She reached out and squeezed Ali's hand, a silent understanding between the new friends.

Chapter Fourteen

The beach was almost empty. Blair had been right when she had suggested this place to Ali. They had been talking about taking Susan to the coast, another item on her list of things to do once more.

The weather was great, warm and sunny with just a light breeze. The drive had been just a couple of hours and Susan had slept on the back seat while Blair had kept Ali company up front. They chatted aimlessly about everything and nothing.

"We used to come here when I was a kid," Blair replied to Ali's question. "My mom would borrow my uncle's car and we'd throw our things in the back and just drive until we got here."

"Sounds like you had fun."

"Yeah, she always made sure we enjoyed every minute." Blair spoke wistfully as she thought about her own mother. She gazed out of the window as Ali drove. "Time is all we really have, isn't it?"

Ali chanced a glance across the car at her friend. "I'm sorry I was such a bitch to you." Blair turned to look at her. She smiled, acknowledging her words before turning back to look out through the window again. Ali finally understood that Blair got it.

~***~

"Do you wanna go sit on the sand?" Ali asked Susan once they had unloaded the car and had a cup of coffee.

"Oh yes, that would be wonderful," she replied, wrapping her arms around her wife's waist and rising up on tiptoes to kiss her smiling lips.

"I'll get it all set up then, do you want to get changed?"

"Ok, I'll meet you out there."

Ali dragged blankets, cushions, and an inflatable chair outside and found a good spot. Blair helped her bring a cooler filled with drinks and snacks.

"I can finish off here if you wanted to go and get changed," Blair said, pointing to the spot they were fixing.

"Sure?"

Blair nodded.

"Ok, thank you. And then you'll join us, right?"

"Oh no, she has that look in her eye. This is the time she wants to spend with you, Ali." She winked.

~***~

Susan was lying in the sunshine on the blanket when Ali finally walked out of the house and onto the sand. She heard a whistle as Blair intimated how 'hot' she looked. The whistle caused Susan to sit up and turn her head. She bit her lip as she watched her wife saunter down the sand in just a peach bikini that she hadn't seen before.

"Are you trying to kill me?" Susan joked. Blair giggled and had to admit that Ali in a bikini was a pretty impressive sight.

"I think she might kill me," Blair admitted, as Ali looked back and forth between them both.

"Oh, both crushing on me now, huh?" Ali stood her ground and then egged them on. "Come on then, get a good long look." She elongated the word "long" and, with a smirk, began a slow, sexy twirl. "Y'all good now?" She winked as both women nodded and grinned.

"I think I might go take a quick dip, cool off," Blair said, fanning herself with her hand.

Susan and Ali both giggled and Susan wrapped herself around Ali as soon as she sat on the ground next to her.

"Wanna make out while we have the place to ourselves?" Susan asked.

"Like I could ever turn you down," Ali answered, checking out her wife's slimmed-down body in her one-piece. She wore a cap on her head and sunglasses, as her eyes had been super sensitive to the light that day. They kissed thoroughly, Susan unable to keep her fingers from trailing the naked skin available.

"God, you're so sexy," she said breathlessly as the kiss broke.

"You just say that so you can get in my pants."

"That's so true!" Susan laughed as she settled back into Ali's arms, leaning her back against Ali's firm breasts. They sat that way for a few minutes, enjoying the contentment both felt together, watching Blair splash about in the water. "I wanna go in the water."

"You can't," Ali whispered in her ear.

"Why not?" Susan twisted herself to look up at Ali.

"Because it will be cold and you can get sick."

"I already am sick, what's a sniffle going to do?" she argued.

"Well, I don't know. Wait until Blair comes back and you can ask her," Ali replied.

"But, I wanna go in the ocean. Just one more time, I want to feel the water against my skin. I promise not for long." She turned in her seat again and gave Ali her best pleading look.

"I guess I can't really argue with that, can I?" She stood and helped Susan to her feet. Once she was up, she scooped her up into her arms and began the short walk to the shoreline.

"Thank you." Susan spoke sincerely.

"I might not like it, Susan, but I will do anything you ask me to," Ali said in reply. It was a decision she had come to a while ago. The only thing she would argue was anything that might give them more time.

They reached the water's edge and Blair walked towards them, a questioning look on her face. Ali smiled sadly, and Blair understood. As she passed, Blair leaned in and whispered, "Not too long, ok?"

Ali nodded and continued to walk into the water. "You want me to carry you in or put you down to walk in?"

"Carry me, is it cold?"

"A little yeah, I'll warn you when—"

"No, no warning. I just want to feel it," Susan said, her arms wrapping tighter around Ali's strong neck.

The water was actually warmer once you were in it and accustomed to it, but the initial feeling when it touched your hot skin was that of freezing. As Ali got to waist height and the water just touched Susan's butt, she screamed like a child with excitement. Her grip tightened around Ali's neck as she attempted to climb Ali and raise herself away from the cold. She was grinning and living in the moment.

"You ready?" Ali asked, a glint of mischief in her eye.

"Ready? For what?"

Ali didn't answer with words. Her eyes sparkled while she bent her knees and dunked them both under the salty water before standing upright once more. Over and over she bounced down and up again, making her wife screech with delight until Ali noticed her shivering and immediately turned them both around to walk quickly back up the beach. Blair met them halfway with dry towels to wrap around Susan and keep her warm. In that moment, Susan's face was alive with joy.

~***~

They spent the evening on the sand around a campfire, toasting marshmallows and making s'mores. Susan sat cross-legged between Ali's thighs, with Ali's arms reaching around her, holding the long stick with the soft mallow impaled on the end of the fire. The flames licked at the edges and turned them brown and a little crispy.

It was while they were sitting there, laughing about how they should have been eating s'mores more often, that Susan suddenly stopped laughing, her eyes rolled back, and her body jerked spasmodically. Every muscle stiffened and shook as Ali held on helplessly.

"Blair!" Ali called out into the darkness, unsure what she should do or what was happening. "*Blair*, please!"

In seconds, the nurse came running from the house, skidding to a halt beside them. It was obvious to her trained eye what was happening, and so she jumped into action without a thought, positioning Susan so that she was as comfortable and safe as she could be.

"She's having a seizure," Blair explained calmly. "We just need to ride it out and keep her from harming herself while she's in it." Blair instructed Ali to twist slightly so that Susan was able to kick out her legs, but she kept her arm under her head in case she banged it against the hard sand beneath them.

The fit was over quite quickly, and other than feeling very tired, Susan felt fine. She tried to downplay the fussing, but Ali carried her up to the house and placed her gently on the couch regardless. She crawled into the space behind Susan, a cocoon of arms and legs as she wrapped them both in a bubble of safety.

"Why's this happening?" Ali asked as Susan slept in her arms, exhausted.

"It's the tumour in her brain Ali, as it gets larger or changes shape, moves, it begins to cause problems, like with her eyesight," Blair explained gently. "Ali, this will most likely happen more often."

"What else is going to happen?" she asked Blair softly, stroking her wife's head.

"Everyone is different, but the blindness could get worse, become permanent. The seizures could become more frequent. She might lose her speech or forget things."

"I hate this, I hate that I can't do anything to make this better."

"Ali, everything you do makes it better. If she didn't have you she would have given up a long time ago. You are what gets her through this. She loves you, Ali."

"It's not enough, loving someone. It's never enough," Ali said sadly.

Chapter Fifteen

Radiation therapy and chemotherapy together for two weeks really took its toll on Susan. The tiredness and illness she would suffer bouts of for a few days during her first cycles were now an everyday occurrence, albeit not quite on the scale of previous bouts. In all, it was exhausting, and her body did very little before it required sleep. She woke often to the sounds of Ali and Blair talking. Sometimes she could even hear the sounds of laughter, and she hoped that it was a sign that Ali would be fine eventually. Of course, she knew and expected Ali would hold onto her hurt for as long as possible, refusing to let it go in case it meant letting Susan go, but in the moments between wakefulness and sleep, when Blair had managed to make her smile or laugh, she knew deep down that it would be possible.

Ali came in from her morning run just as Susan and Blair were setting up the couch for a day of television and napping. Susan was sitting upright, plump pillows at her back and side so her frail frame could be supported comfortably. There was a side table adorned with everything she might need, from water and her tablets to snacks and her iPod.

"Hey, you're all sweaty," she laughed as Ali attempted to kiss her good morning.

"Ha, like you ever complained before!"

"Yes, well I was usually as sweaty then, so it didn't matter." She smiled softly, not meaning a word of it, and Ali knew it. She bent lower once more and kissed her again, a soft gentle press of lips against lips. "Mm, I do so love kissing you," Susan said dreamily, her eyes still closed as she memorised the feel, the taste of her wife.

"Course you do, I am the best kisser in town," she joked, but her mind also went to a place where kissing her wife could be stored.

"Go have a shower and then come sit with me, I want to tell you something."

Ali raised a brow, aware that telling her something could mean absolutely anything, and not always something she wanted to hear.

~***~

Washed, dressed, and looking somewhat human again, Ali made her way back downstairs to find Susan asleep once more. She smiled at the sight and took a quick trip to the kitchen to pour some coffee. She had gotten used to having Blair here. Usually, she had lived with instant coffee, but Blair made a pot every morning and Ali enjoyed it to the fullest.

"I'll miss this when you're gone," Ali said absently to Blair as she joined her at the dining table.

"Our whimsical chats or my coffee?"

"The coffee, most definitely the coffee." She pulled a chair out and sat down. Both women could easily see Susan from where they were seated. "She's a lot more tired lately." It was a statement rather than a question.  .

"Yes, the treatments really take it out of them, and of course the illness does the same so..." She left the sentence unfinished.

"I know she wants to stop the treatments. I just can't find a way to be okay with that. Selfish, huh?" Ali said, taking a sip of her coffee, her eyes never leaving her wife's sleeping form. She looked so small, so frail, and childlike.

"Nope, not selfish at all. We all want to know we have done all we can, we all want the time together to be endless," Blair said. She reached out and took Ali's hand in hers. "She understands."

"Tell me and be honest, do you think her having these treatments is going to make any difference?"

"Ali, I can't tell you yes or no, but what I can tell you is that she is one of the most courageous women I have nursed. She doesn't give up, but yes, she might not be so exhausted without them. She won't feel so unwell."

"So, she is suffering because of the treatments?" Ali spoke quietly, her brow creased. "Am I making her suffer?"

"You're not making her do anything. She is choosing to do it."

"But, she is still suffering?"

"Yes, it isn't fun for anyone. But Ali, even if she stops the treatment, she will still be in pain. A lot of pain."

"And they can manage that though, right? I mean, she can take a bunch of painkillers and—"

Blair nodded and smiled sadly. It was tough, deciding one way or another. Keep doing one treatment or try something else, or accept the inevitable and allow it to happen. That was hard.

Susan stirred on the couch and Ali got up instantly. She walked the distance across the room, her smile brightening as Susan caught her gaze and grinned up at her.

"Hey lazybones," Ali said quietly. Perching on the edge of the settee, she gently lifted her wife's legs so she could sit down, placing them on her lap and gently running her hand up and down the length of them. Her bony knees created an obstacle. "How are you feeling?"

"Tired mostly." Susan yawned.

"But how are you really feeling, babe?" Ali asked, her eyes glistening. Susan looked at her; their eyes held as she understood what Ali was asking her.

"I feel ready. I feel as though my time is nearing, and I want to—" She didn't want to say the word "stop;" she never wanted to stop. "I don't want to continue like this, Ali."

Ali felt herself nodding, and without looking, she knew she would see tears in those big green eyes as they looked at her.

"Then make me a promise," Ali said, turning to look at her, taking her hands in her own. "You stop all your treatments, but you promise me you won't just give up?"

Susan smiled. "I promise I will never just give up. And now, you make me a promise."

"What is it?"

"You promise me that when I am gone, you won't give up either." She saw Ali tense, her jaw tighten. "You won't give up on finding love again."

"I can't promise that," Ali said, shaking her head from side to side.

"Yes, you can. I know you, Alison Jane Jenkins, and I know if you make me this promise you will keep it."

"That's why I can't make it."

"Not right now, but in a year maybe, two at the most. Promise me that you will let someone into your heart again."

"Nope, I can't. You can't ask me to do that Susan, that's not fair."

"It's what I want, it's my last act of love. When you meet her, and you will, you let her in. Promise me."

Ali took a deep breath, trying to steady herself.

"If?"

"When." Susan insisted.

"If I meet someone, I promise I will do my best to let her in."

"Ok well, that's more than I thought I would get out of you, so I'll take that." Susan smiled and pulled her wife into her.

Chapter Sixteen

Susan's death came early one summer morning when the sky was a cerulean blue, the clouds were sparse, and the air was still. It had been several weeks since she had stopped her treatments, and for the most part, she had felt much better about herself. She still became exhausted after any activity, but she was able to take part at least, and that had thrilled her.

They went to the park and had picnics, fed the ducks. Even though her last few days meant using a wheelchair more and more, she didn't mind so much because, by the grace of God, she still had her mind, her speech. Her biggest fear had been that she would forget Ali, or lose her ability to communicate.

Ali took her to the zoo to see the monkeys. They went out in the car for drives, to nowhere in particular; just the two of them and the car driving around the places they used to go, like the school they went to and old friends' houses. They watched movies with popcorn and ate ice cream.

Time together had been magical and wondrous, and they had found the words they needed to say all the things that needed saying.

With Blair's help, and the medication that constantly changed to fit her needs, they were able to keep as normal a life as possible for quite a few weeks, but eventually, Susan had to admit she wasn't up to doing much more than being carried downstairs to the couch. Her blindness came and went more often until in her last days it appeared to be permanent. The seizures happened more and more frequently, and Ali was terrified that one of them would be the reason Susan passed, but that wasn't the way it was meant to be.

On that bright summer's morning at just gone 10 a.m., Susan lay snuggled with Ali on the settee talking about a day many years ago, a million and one memories they shared. When Ali finished speaking, expecting a reply from Susan, there was none. She glanced down, and at first, she thought Susan had simply dozed off again. The realisation that she was gone came moments later.

She had taken her last breath while watching Ali smile and laugh about their life together. She had known in her last months, weeks, days, and minutes that she was loved; and that, at the end, was all that mattered.

~***~

Blair helped Ali with the funeral arrangements and stayed on for several more days caring for Ali. Susan had asked her right at the start if she was prepared to do that because she knew her wife would need someone at home taking care of the important things, like eating and getting dressed. Susan had done a lot of thinking and organising in her last months. Right up until the last moment, she was herself.

"Ali, do you want me to organise those donations that have come in?" Blair asked. Their friends had, on request, sent money and cheques with the cards of condolences rather than send flowers to the funeral. Most people had arranged an online donation and sent a card with the details written inside, along with their best wishes and regrets, but some, the older members of the family for instance, had preferred the old-fashioned way. Ali didn't mind; Susan would have laughed about it.

"Oh, uh yes, please, if you don't mind. I'm just about to head down to the florist to—" She noticed a letter had arrived addressed to herself. She picked up the envelope and studied the writing. It was Susan's handwriting. "I'll just be at the florist's," she said again, placing the envelope into the inside pocket of her jacket.

The mourners gathered at St Luke's church on the corner of Meadow Lane and Dewhurst at 11 a.m. The sky was a mottled blue, clouds passing by on the breeze that blew steadily. They wore smart dresses and shirts, in every colour imaginable. There was nobody wearing black. Just the way that Susan had wanted.

The hearse arrived carrying just the coffin and a single bouquet of orange and pink flowers.

Ali arrived in a pink Cadillac, as requested by Susan, with her parents and Susan's mother. She wore a green dress that would have matched perfectly with Susan's eyes. Susan had picked it out for her on their last shopping trip. At the graveside, Ali felt a hand slip into hers and looked around to see Blair standing next to her. As she scanned the area, she realised everyone else had already left. It was peaceful, quiet. On any other day, she might have enjoyed it.

"How long have I been standing here?" she asked, her sense of time something she had lost all track of recently.

"Oh, only about twenty-three minutes," she said, looking at her watch. "But who's counting?" She smiled softly. "You ready to go, or you need a few more minutes?"

She took one last look at the pine coffin several feet below. Its metal inscription to the body that it cocooned sparkled as the sunlight bounced off it. Beside it was a smattering of earth and some single roses that had been thrown in by her friends and relations. She imprinted the image to memory and then nodded to Blair. They walked slowly, Blair linking their arms as they talked in quiet whispers.

~***~

When the last mourner had gone and Blair had wished her goodnight, Ali poured herself a double scotch and took it outside to the porch. She sat in the hammock and pulled from her pocket the letter that had arrived several days earlier.

She looked at it over and over in her hand, brought it to her nose and inhaled the scent of her wife. Peeling back the seal with the utmost care so as to preserve it perfectly, she opened it.

It contained just a single sheet of paper, the kind you found in copiers and printers. It was dated three weeks previously. She wondered how Susan had managed to post it without her knowledge but then smiled to herself. Blair.

She pulled the paper from its sheath and took a breath, preparing herself for her wife's real last words. She felt the trickle of tears before she had even read the first word. The slow wet stream slid naturally down her cheek in the path of so many previous trails.

My dearest Ali,

A promise is a promise, I kept mine and fought for as long as I could. Now you must keep yours. Know always that I love you, I always have and I always will, that will never change. So, keep your promise my darling and let someone else be as lucky as I was to be loved by you. Let someone else love you just as much as I do.

Get up each day and live it as though it was your last. Go out and meet new people, surround yourself with fun and happiness. Try new things!

Think often of me, but not so much that you can't move forward. I never held you back in life and I won't hold you back now I am gone. Honour me in death as you did in life.

Take care of yourself, my love.

I love you.

Susan xxx

She had the letter framed, but only after taking a copy that she folded neatly and carried with her in her wallet. One day she found Blair reading it in its place on the wall. She had a tear on her cheek and whispered that it was beautiful. Ali felt happier for some unknown reason, knowing Blair loved it just as much as she did.

Ali took the box she had hidden that contained Susan's hair and found a jeweller who could make glass pendants that incorporated some of the locks. She had several made in different styles and wore a different one each day. She bought extra bottles of Susan's favourite perfume and placed them all inside a beautiful wooden trunk. As she cleared through Susan's things, she found items of jewellery, her hairbrush, a lipstick. The last book she read and never finished. Her bucket list. Diaries and notebooks she had written anything in. Several videotapes of holidays and parties they had attended, taken when Susan was alive and vibrant, captured for eternity. She had them put onto discs. She kept the negligee Susan wore the last time they made love.

Everything went carefully into the trunk. The trunk went into their bedroom.

~***~

Her colleagues had surprised her on her return to work with a canvas collage they had designed with photographs of Susan and Ali. She had it hung in her office to the side of her desk where she could see it anytime she wanted to, right next to the letter she had had copied for her office.

For four more weeks, Blair stayed and helped her organise everything she needed to do. They spent many evenings talking long into the night. It helped Ali to have someone there, someone who understood. Their friends and their family all stopped by and visited, but they never quite got what the last 6 months had been like for Ali and Susan. Oh, they came and saw Susan when she was up to it, but she always put on a show for them, always tried to shield them from the reality of it all. So it helped Ali that she had Blair to cry with, laugh with, and lean on in those first few weeks.

But like everything, time was interrupted. There was someone else in need of Blair's expertise, somebody else whose life was coming to an end, and so Blair packed her things and moved out of the place that had become a home to her for the last half a year.

On the day she left, Ali made sure to be home. She gave her a bouquet of beautiful flowers and a card. She thanked her profusely and then handed her a small box. Blair opened it to find one of the pendants that Ali had had made.

"To remember her by," Ali said, both women standing on the threshold. To think all those months ago when Ali had come home to find this woman here, she had been angry, and now as she was about to leave, she was sad.

"Thank you, it's beautiful, but I will never forget her, Ali." She leant forward and kissed Ali on the cheek, and they squeezed hands. "Or you. Take care."

Ali walked into the house, alone for the first time in 13 years.

# Part Two

Chapter One

Work had been hectic. Ali had just finished her fourth 15-hour day in a row, and she was exhausted. Life had been busy for her and she was glad of that. Busy kept her mind focused, kept her bank account full, and made sure she didn't have to think about anything other than work.

Arriving home, she was greeted as usual by Jasper, the cat from next door. He hopped down off the fence and sauntered down the path, his tail waving back and forth in the air as he gained on her. She reached down and petted him like she always did.

"Hello Jasper, how are you today?" The cat twisted his head so his other ear got as much attention as the first. She assumed this meant he had had a good day. "Well, I need to go inside now and try to find something to eat. I'll see you this time tomorrow, shall I?" He rolled over and onto the ground, submitting to her completely. She knew, of course, that it was a trap. The moment she went to stroke the tummy on offer, he would pounce. She had learned that lesson a long time ago. Susan used to laugh at her every time she fell for it. She would come inside the house cursing and act like a baby over a few scratches, and Susan would find the first aid box.

*"I don't know why you insist on trying to rub his tummy, you know he only does it so he can catch you," Susan would say in all seriousness, but behind it all would be those smiling eyes she couldn't hide when it came to Ali.*

*"I know, I need a protector," Ali would answer back as she watched Susan clean and dress her wounds. Once Susan had finished, she would rise up onto tiptoes and kiss her.*

*"That's why you've got me. All better?" It was almost worth the scratches.*

She boiled the kettle and found a clean mug in the cupboard, feeling thankful for Mrs Jeffries' cleaning service that sent a nice young lady and occasionally a nice gentleman around to give her home the going-over it required once a week.

With a steaming cup of coffee made, she kicked off her heels and made her way to their bedroom. She placed the coffee cup on one of the comical coasters that had ended up in here after Susan had had a prolonged few days in bed. For no real reason it had never been put back and now, she kind of liked it here.

Her clothes came off, tossed aside without a further thought, and she stepped into the shower to wash another day away. Wrapped in a towel, she walked back into the bedroom and took a sip of the now much cooler coffee. Her phone beeped and she picked it up to check the screen. A new email from her secretary.

It was past 11 p.m.; it could wait until the morning.

She towelled off and pulled on a pair of old pyjama bottoms Susan had bought one birthday for her. They were plain and comfortable, warm and cosy, just the way she liked them. She pulled on a white t-shirt. Susan's white t-shirt; she had kept five of her shirts to sleep in. Her scent was long gone. She picked up the perfume bottle that was Susan's favourite, giving herself a tiny spritz. In an instant she was surrounded by Susan once more. The coffee was cold, but it didn't matter now, and so she snuggled down into the pillows and inhaled deeply, drifting off to sleep with a sadness she never could quite shift.

During those first weeks and months, her dreams would be invaded constantly by Susan. Ali would wake, and for those first few sacred seconds, she would forget. Smiling, she would open her eyes and look across the pillow expecting to see pretty green eyes staring back at her. For the rest of the day, she would feel numb as her brain registered the loss again.

Gradually over time, the dreams lessened, and when she did have dreams about Susan, she would savour them, try and hold onto the feelings and words she felt and heard while she slumbered.

~***~

The last year had been a rollercoaster of emotions for Ali Jenkins. Every time she felt as though she were moving forwards, something would happen that made it all come crashing down on her once more. There was just no escaping the absolute sadness that she felt. The loss was just too immense.

Those first lonely weeks surrounded by everyone that wanted to share in her grief were the longest of her life. In comparison, her life with Susan had been a blur. So quickly had it passed them by that now it just didn't seem like they had had any time together, and yet she knew they had.

Her heart understood just how much time they had had together. Her heart understood just how deeply Susan was ingrained in her psyche, her life. And that was why it hurt so much still.

Her colleagues, the people that worked for her, had taken up the mantle, and between them, they had kept the business thriving. She would forever be grateful to each and every one of them.

They had known Susan and were grieving her in their own ways, but it wasn't the same for them, and they understood as best they could why some days Ali would throw herself into her work. She would be in the office before any of them arrived and be the last to leave each night. They had noticed the change. Ali had gone from being bright and breezy to dull and listless. Her desk, which once upon a lifetime ago had been immaculate and organised, was now a dishevelled space full of paper and drawings. She was snappy and irritable, but they accepted it, hoping that one day their Ali would return.

Weeks had quickly turned into months, months of lying around the house in Susan's t-shirt and a pair of old jogging pants that had seen better days even before Susan had passed.

*"You do know you can afford to buy a new pair of these, don't you?" Susan had laughed, holding up the offending pants and looking at Ali through the hole in the knee.*

*"Yes, but why would I? They're just so comfortable now that I've broken them in." She smirked and made a grab for them.*

*"Uh uh uh." She giggled as she yanked them away from Ali's reach. "If you want them then you'll have to do better than that." She held them behind her back and pouted, lips puckered for a kiss she knew would be forthcoming.*

Eventually, something lifted just enough that Ali began to feel a little more her old self. The cloud that followed her was a little less dark, a little less...suffocating, and her colleagues were just a little bit relieved as life in the office became a little more fun again. Ali was able to smile once more, find humour in a joke or just sit and enjoy a conversation. She was working long hours still, but her desk was tidy again.

As the anniversary of the first year approached, everyone braced themselves. Ali stayed home of course, but there was an understanding between everyone at the office that one of them would take on the responsibility of popping in and making sure that Ali was ok.

And that's just what they did. For a full week, each day one of them would arrive with lunch or dinner and spend a few hours making small talk. Between them all, they got her through it.

Chapter Two

The office at 7 a.m. was a pretty quiet affair most mornings, and something Ali both enjoyed and hated all at once. She was the only one there until Jack arrived around eight, and the silence was often asphyxiating.

By nine o'clock the office would be a flurry of activity. Fi and Sara would bicker over which idea they liked best, and the office would come alive. Ola will be running around trying to keep everyone happy with the food she cooked the night before, and Ali's secretary Paula would be chasing her to reply to the numerous emails she sent her the day before or possibly days ago. But for the next hour she would struggle to keep her focus, and often her mind would wander back to Susan, to the life they had; that she had had.

*"Are you moping again?" Susan would say.*

*"No, I don't mope," Ali would laugh.*

*"Oh you do, you can't fool me, Ali Jane." She only ever called her Ali Jane when she was being playful. "Don't you have some work to do?"*

She pulled up a file on her screen and began to move the graphics around, playing with colours and images. Her company specialised in company branding, everything from letterheads to signage. She had started her career originally in advertising, working on magazine ads and poster campaigns, but found she had a bigger passion and a greater eye for the branding side of the industry. Buildings, she loved buildings and being able to dress them and make them stand out with the right signage. Lighting and information were what she was most passionate about.

"Morning boss," Jack said, his bald head poking around the door, a hand held out waggling a mug. "Coffee?" The hour had flown by. It used to drag; in those first few months after Susan passed, these hours by herself would feel like a lifetime, but now they sped up. She wasn't sure what that meant, but she had noticed the change.

"Hey Jack, yes, please. I would love one," she answered. As he turned and began to walk toward the small kitchen, she rose from her seat and followed him down the short hall that linked everything in the office. "Did you get my email last night? I'm sorry it was so late, but I didn't get the information until the last minute," she said, his back still to her.

"Yes, thanks. I'll be right on it as soon as I've had one of these." He turned, held the coffee jug up high, and then turned back to pour two mugs, adding milk to hers before he passed it across.

"That's fine, I just wanted to make sure you got it."

"Morning." Another voice from behind. "And yes please!" Paula called over her shoulder as she went straight to her office to drop her bag on the desk and set up for the day.

Ali followed her with an extra cup. Paula's mug read 'cup of sunshine first, or back off!'

"Aw thanks, Ali. God, I need this," Paula said, smiling as usual. The dark-skinned women had a joyful way about her pretty much 24/7, unless she didn't get her coffee of course. She was an attractive woman in her twenties with two kids at home and a husband who had served his country for fifteen years. He had been medically discharged the year before and was struggling to find permanent work, but it never got Paula down. Ali often wondered how she did it, kept her spirits high when she must be under so much stress at times, but at least she still had him.

"Busy night?"

"It wasn't so bad, Keenan didn't want to go to bed until Daddy got home, which was way past his bedtime, and way past mine, and of course that meant that Gracie didn't want to go to bed until Keenan did." Ali smiled at the thought of her assistant's young children. They were cute; whenever Paula brought them by the office, they had Ali wrapped around their little fingers.

"If he was mine, he would be up all night every night, I wouldn't be able to say no to him." Ali laughed and moved toward her own office.

"Oh, trust me! That cuteness soon wears off," Paula called out. "Did you get that last-minute addition to your diary?"

"Uh, nope, I don't think I did," Ali said, walking back to the outer office. "What was it?" she asked, completely forgetting about the late email.

Paula was sitting at her desk, glasses now perched on her nose as she stared attentively at the screen in front of her. "You have a new 10:30 a.m. appointment, a Miss Barnes from Promise Hills."

"Hmm ok, well I'd best get on with what I have to do first, otherwise I won't be doing anything other than running around like a headless chicken!" She smiled and turned on her heels. "Do not disturb unless the building is on fire."

"Yes boss," Paula chuckled to herself.

Chapter Three

"Ali, your 10:30 is here, shall I send Miss Barnes in?" Paula's voice rang out over the office intercom. Ali pressed the button to reply. "Uh yes. Thank you, Paula, give me one minute and then show her in please." She released the button and then rose from her desk, ready to greet her potential new client. Smoothing down invisible creases in her outfit, she picked at a few bits of imaginary fluff.

*"You look fine, stop worrying. It's just my parents,"* Susan's voice whispered against her ear.

*"I know, and I know I have met them before, but I wasn't sleeping with you then."*

*"You're not sleeping much now either."* She winked.

She caught sight of her reflection in the large mirror that hung to her left. Her dark hair was a little shorter after her last visit to the salon. She wasn't sure if she liked it or not, but it would grow back, so she wasn't going to worry about it too much. She looked tired and a little gaunt still, but she was starting to feel more like her old self at last.

A cool shiver ran across her shoulders and down her spine, so much so that she turned to check the window was closed. She felt herself calm just as the door opened and her secretary stepped inside, moving to the left to allow Miss Barnes to enter.

"Miss Barnes to see you, Ali." Ali turned back around to acknowledge the client only to get the shock of her life.

"Blair?" She stood open-mouthed as she looked straight into the face of the woman who had nursed Susan through her illness. "Oh my goodness, how are you?" Ali said, coming around the desk to embrace her.

"Hi Ali, I am well, thank you. You look great," Blair replied as they broke apart.

"God, I do not. I look like someone that hasn't had a good night's sleep for a lifetime." She laughed heartily. "Wow, I can't believe it." She took a step back and really looked at Blair. She looked so different now. She was dressed in a form-fitting suit jacket with matching skirt, and the blouse she wore was a beautiful cerise pink. She wore heels too, not the white pumps she always used to wear. She looked every inch the businesswoman, not a palliative care nurse. In the centre of her chest, the pendant hung loosely. "You look fabulous, Blair."

Paula tapped on the door gently before entering with a tray full of coffee and pastries, the usual fare for an in-house meeting.

"Thank you, Paula, just place them on the table, please. You can take a break if you want to." She was still grinning and, Paula noted, holding the new client's hands.

"O-kay." She raised a humorous eyebrow and stifled a small giggle before backing out of the room quietly.

"So, oh goodness, please take a seat," Ali said. She led them to a small sitting area and then returned to bring the tray over and settled them both onto the comfortable couch. "How have you been?"

"Good, really good actually."

"Excellent, so what are you doing now? You don't look like a nurse!" Ali smiled, a smile that actually reached her eyes, something that didn't happen often anymore.

"I...No, well kind of...before I came to work for Susan—" She recognised the pain that flickered briefly across Ali's face but continued on. "I had been trying to organise something I have kind of been dreaming of doing for a long time, I just never had the funds to do it." Ali poured them both a coffee. "When I left you to go and work for my next client, I got to talking with her daughter and well, I told her about my idea and she agreed to be a backer for me. I got some money together myself and a few other people on board and here I am, the proud owner and manager of Promise Hills retreat hospice." Ali noticed that while Blair talked, she fingered the pendant around her neck. She wondered if Blair had worn it especially today or if she always wore it, like the matching one around her own neck.

"Oh God, Blair that is amazing." She offered a pastry, but Blair declined and took a sip of her drink instead. "So, what can I do for you?"

"I was hoping I could persuade you to take on our branding. The building is almost complete, and we need the area to have proper customized signage, and well, I remembered this is what you do and so, here I am," Blair said with a huge smile. It really was good to see Ali again and to see she was doing ok. She had worried about her the first few weeks, but she was so busy with her next client that she had barely any time even to sleep, and she also didn't want to intrude. Ali had never really been happy with her being in their life, and although they had come to an understanding along the way, it was never her job to linger in the clients' partners' lives, regardless of how much she liked them.

"Of course, that's what we do." Touching Blair's arm, she nodded and said, "I would be honoured to help you with your design. Did you have any ideas of what you wanted yet?"

"No, not really." She laughed nervously, "Completely out of my comfort zone, to be honest."

"Okay, well look, this is what I do, and I am pretty good at it so, can I come along and take a look at the building, have a chat on site and get a feel for the place?"

"Of course, that would be perfect. I knew coming to you would be the right choice," Blair said, gushing a little; she really was glad to see Ali again.

Chapter Four

The hospice was set in a beautiful part of town, on the outskirts, but close enough that relatives and friends would be able to visit easily. The backdrop of trees and fields made it feel as though you were miles away in the countryside somewhere peaceful and quiet. Susan would have loved it. As she slowly drove up towards the large building ahead of her, she could imagine the tranquillity a place like this would bring to someone like Susan. She parked her car to one side, as there were no formal parking areas just yet, and was greeted by Blair and her site manager, Joel.

It was an old manor house that had been gutted in a fire several years previously, so they had managed to buy the house and the land at a steal. Now, however, the last areas of rejuvenation were taking place, and so Ali stood outside in her made-to-measure black pantsuit and her Manolo Blahniks with a bright yellow hard hat on her head and a hi-vis jacket on her back. Other than their hair colour, the two women matched each other perfectly.

They went from room to room with Blair excitedly explaining each room's reason for being. The light and airy main living space was a communal area where patients and staff could get together for those who wanted the company of others. There was to be a music room that would be home to a piano, guitars, and other musical equipment. Music was one of the most important aspects of therapy; it soothed people and helped to take them back to memories of better times.

Blair was animated as she explained about the opportunity to have musicians and artists come in and spend time with residents. At the end of the corridor was a library that would house a small internet café area too; they wanted to create a sense of normality for the residents. Ali observed her for a moment. Her enthusiasm was inspirational.

The upper rooms, which were all serviced by elevators large enough to wheel a bed into, were all to be furnished bedrooms. Each room on the second floor would have its own bathroom and be for people with specialist palliative care at the very end of their life cycle, but on the third floor the rooms where slightly larger and would house a small kitchenette and living space for those still a little more independent.

Outside sat a large, imposing building set to the side of the main house that was being fitted with an indoor swimming pool, sauna, Jacuzzi, and gym.

"Blair, this place is amazing!" Ali spoke from the heart as she turned back and forth to take it all in.

"Really? You really like it?" Blair said. She had been biting her lip nervously throughout most of the tour. Impressing Ali had been important to her; an ex-client would either see this building for what she hoped it would be or point out the flaws.

"Yes, what isn't to like? I think your residents will find a lot of enjoyment in their last days here, Blair, and with your expert care I know they will be in good hands." She took Blair's hand and held it firmly as she spoke, their eyes locked together as she added, "I know Susan would agree with me."

"I am just so...I've had these dreams ya know, but I never thought that one day..." She looked to the sky for guidance. "That one day I would be able to do this and be able to help more than one person at a time."

"Blair, what you do is amazing. I know in the beginning I was so very hesitant about you being there." She chuckled as she took Blair by the elbow and guided her back outside to where her car was parked. "Without you, I would not have coped at all, and Susan's last days would have ended up with her trying to placate me rather than doing all the things she was able to do."

"Thank you for saying that, but I think you did a fantastic job of coping. Not everybody does, and look at you now," she answered as they reached Ali's red Audi.

"Oh, I wouldn't say that, I guess I am still coping. Each day is still a struggle, it's just a little less." Her smile saddened. She looked away and blinked back the tears. "See?" she laughed. "Still crying."

Blair pulled her into a hug and held her until she composed herself again. It felt good to have someone hold her once more; she had missed being held.

"Ha, not quite the impression I like to give my clients!" Ali chuckled again as she pulled back from the embrace. She was never quite sure how to react when people hugged her now. It felt so alien.

"Well, I would like to think maybe we're more friends than clients," Blair said, her smile broad and warm.

"Yes, and my firm would like to do this work pro bono."

"What? No, you can't—"

"Actually Blair, I can, and I want to. It's a thank you from Susan and myself." She beeped the car alarm off and opened the driver's door. "I'll call later about another meeting to discuss colour schemes and materials." As she climbed into the car, Blair called her name.

"Ali? Thank you, your generosity means we can maybe employ another member of staff."

"You're welcome." She slid into the leather seat and closed the door, her mind swirling with images of Susan.

*"That was a lovely gesture," Susan said. Ali had just paid for a stressed-out young mother's coffee. She had been searching her bag for her wallet, her child screaming, everyone scowling at her for holding them up and for having to deal with the noise of the child.*

*"No, it was the right thing to do, she looked like she needed something nice to happen today," Ali replied as she sipped her*

*frappe. They were sitting outside in the sunshine, holding hands and just enjoying each other like they always did.*

*"Like I said sweetheart, it was a lovely gesture, one that might earn you a fun night." She grinned.*

There was a knocking noise. She shook herself out of her reminiscence and looked to her left. Blair stood by the window, bent low, indicating she should lower the window.

"You ok?" she asked as soon as the gap between them opened up.

"Oh, yes fine, thank you," Ali answered quickly. She pulled the belt around herself and clipped it into place. "I'll speak to you later then." Blair nodded with a smile, a concerned smile. Ali pulled slowly away and watched through the rear-view mirror as Blair grew smaller.

Chapter Five

"Oh my god," stated Jack, one word emphasised as much as the next. Fi waltzed into the kitchen, her latest fashion ensemble being a pair of hot pants in neon pink with bright yellow tights and bright green knee-length boots. "What on earth did you see when you looked in the mirror?

"Oh no," Ola began. "In the words of my very Nigerian grandmother, 'When the mouse laughs at the cat, he had better hope there is a hole nearby'." She laughed hard with Paula joining in. Ali smiled at the scene in front of her and, like the others awaited Fiona's reply. She stood, hand on hip, eyebrow raised, waiting for them to finish.

"What I see, Jack, is a work of art, not a balding, slightly overweight man in tan," she deadpanned, giving Jack the once-over to make the point. His cheeks blushed and he smiled; the two of them always bantered back and forth. Ali had her suspicions that there was a little bit more to it if either of them cared to admit it, but neither would.

"I happen to like tan," he said, turning on his heels and walking back to his own desk, the grin growing wider.

"Seriously though girl, pink and green should never be seen," Paula said, looking to Ola for support.

"No, that's blue and green, isn't it?" Ola asked.

"Whatever it is, I kind of like it," Ali added. "For a logo maybe." The girls all burst into laughter as Fi gave them all the finger. "Staff meeting in five!" Ali called out before heading to the meeting room.

~***~

The staff members of Jenkins Graphics had become a family of sorts to Ali. Her own family lived a fair distance away, and although she made every effort to see them at least three or four times a year, it was these people that were there for her on a daily basis. But, she had kept them all at arm's length. She loved them all. Each one of them had a unique personality that made them absolutely essential to her business and to her, but she never felt the need to take those relationships any further. It was very rare that she would spend time with any of them outside of work, no matter how hard they tried to include her in things, but she enjoyed hearing about their lives and families all the same.

"Ok, I trust you all had a fabulous weekend and that by the end of the day I will be up to date on any essential gossip to be had, but first things first. Where are we on the Roland Group contract? Ola?"

"All is as it should be, we have the designs being mocked up ready for presentation. Sara has the presentation booked in for the 11th and as far as I am aware, nothing has changed." She looked to Sara, a woman in her early twenties who had impressed

Ali enough when she worked for the firm as an intern that she had offered her a job once she finished her education. She had been working on the Roland Group's design with Ola, and the pair had done an amazing job so far.

"Yes, I have a meeting with Garrett Roland and Paul Donaldson. I expect them to love the design mocks and to sign contracts on the day," Sara announced to the group.

"Great, Paula can you add that to my diary so I don't forget?"

"Already done."

Ali smiled at the woman who ran her life almost as well as Susan.

*"Didn't I tell you last week about that?"*

*"No, I am pretty sure you—" She was about to say "didn't" but swiftly changed it to "did!" She smiled as she found the note on her calendar.*

*"Uh huh, because when have I ever not told you about anything important that you need to know?" Susan said, her arms slipping effortlessly around Ali's neck. She was smiling as she closed the space between their lips.*

*"Uh, well there was that one time when—" Susan began to move away, her eyes narrowing to a squint. "No, you are right, absolutely never forgotten to tell me anything."*

*"That's better." Susan smirked and closed the gap completely.*

"Ali?" Paula touched her arm gently. They were all used to her drifting off somewhere in her head. It happened with less frequency now. At the beginning, when Ali first returned to work, it would be a daily or sometimes even hourly occurrence, but lately, it only happened sporadically.

"Sorry, where were we?" she said, shaking herself visibly from her thoughts.

"Promise Hills?" Jack said. "Who do you want to take the lead on that?"

"Oh, I am," she said instantly. Everyone around the table looked at each other, questioning. "Blair is a friend, she uh, you might remember her, she was Susan's nurse."

"Are you sure you don't want one of us to take it on?" Jack inquired again. Having a daily reminder around the place like Blair Barnes might not be the best thing for their boss. Their concern was evident; they wanted to protect her.

"Yes, I want to do it. I haven't really gotten that deeply involved with anything for a while." She smiled at him and looked around the table at all of the concerned faces staring back at her. "I'll be fine," she insisted.

"Ok." He grinned and twisted back in his chair to face the rest of the room.

Chapter Six

Her bed was big, too big to sleep alone in, which was why she often ended up on the couch, a blanket pulled haphazardly over her. She was excited about the prospect of working on the Promise Hills project. It would do her good to get stuck into something like this for a while, and she was brimming with ideas. Maybe that was why she couldn't quite get to sleep.

The clock on the mantle struck three, a small chime that she usually didn't hear, but lying here in the darkness and the silence, it was as loud as a bell. She tossed and turned, finding a comfortable spot on her side, and in doing so, her eyeline was drawn to the photograph on the shelf, lit by the moonlight that streamed in like a super trouper beam upon it. Thinking back to the day it was taken, she wondered if Susan herself was sending a message.

*"You do know you would be much more comfortable in a bed right now, don't you?" Susan had whispered against the shell her of ear, sending goosebumps across her skin as she pressed herself up against Ali's warm spine.*

*"Yep, but you wanted to go camping," Ali replied, turning on her small, makeshift inflatable bed to face the woman she apparently would do anything for.*

*"I didn't actually think you would agree to it," she admitted, fidgeting about on her own inflatable bed that seemed to be deflating rapidly. She smirked at Ali, leant forward, and placed a kiss on her cheek. "Can we go and find a hotel, where I can ravish you for the rest of the night without the fear of being eaten alive?" Ali had laughed as Susan immediately slapped her shoulder and the annoying pest that was buzzing around her with its high-pitched whine.*

*"Oh, now you agree with me that camping is for teenagers and not grown women?"*

*"I wouldn't say that, I mean last night was fun, wasn't it, watching the stars and being at one with nature?" She winked, remembering just how at one they were with nature. "But, okay, I'm done. I want a bed!" she shrieked, jumping up and down to rid herself of something creepy that she felt sure was crawling up her leg. "Beds are made for sleeping in," Susan insisted.*

She sighed and winced as she felt the muscles ache in her torso, but she got up and dragged herself off to her bedroom, to their bed.

~***~

On the other side of town, Blair lay awake in her own bed. The monkey chatter in her brain just wouldn't shut off. She was making lists, and then lists of lists. There was so much to do and not very much time now before everything needed to come together. So it was no wonder that she couldn't sleep; that's what she told herself.

It was hot in the room, and she kicked the bedclothes off, getting frustrating when the sheet became tangled with her bare legs. She was frustrated a lot lately.

In reality, her mind was awash with images – images of Ali Jenkins. Gorgeous, sexy Ali Jenkins.

She had always been attracted to Ali, there was no way she could deny that to herself. Ali was the kind of woman that was understated. She could have been a model in Blair's opinion, but instead, she had chosen to follow her passions in life. And she loved passionately; who wouldn't be attracted to her?

But she hadn't given it any thought when she had contacted Ali for Promise Hills. In fact, she had forgotten all about her little crush that had developed back when she was nursing Susan; now though, it was all she could think about.

Thinking about Ali caused her heart to race and her mouth to dry. She tried to argue with herself that it was just a ridiculous crush on a beautiful woman, and anyway, Blair had a date soon. She closed her eyes and tried to concentrate on that. The image of Josie popped into her head and was promptly pushed out again by a blue-eyed brunette with a smile that dazzled Blair in every way.

She grabbed the pillow from behind her head and slammed it over her face, groaning out loud in the process. It was going to be a long night, and an even longer day ahead.

Chapter Seven


Blair was still up before the alarm. An early bird for so many years, with her client's needs more important than a good night's sleep, her internal clock would always wake her early regardless.

She was still not quite used to her new morning routine. Gone were the endless cups of coffee to kick-start her day. Gone were the uniforms and comfy shoes, and in their place were power suits and heels. She checked herself in the mirror and still couldn't quite recognise the image that presented itself to her. Her dark blonde hair was tied neatly in a ponytail that swept past the collar of her dark suit jacket and gave the appearance of a confident and stylish young woman.

Having to play the part of a businesswoman was something she was desperate to avoid, but when you needed backers and had things to get done, then you had to do what was necessary. Her meetings with healthcare officials and local government had gone well, and she had been granted all the licenses she needed and had all the right paperwork in place to open Promise Hills as soon as she could organise all of the work on the building to be completed, and she was almost there. The construction was finished, and now only the renovation and decoration were left to do.

With somebody like Ali Jenkins in charge of the signage and design, it made her life a little bit easier; trust in your workforce was key to getting anything completed on time and within budget.

There was the chiming sound of her phone ringing from deep within her bag. She rifled through it and found the noise, swiping the screen quickly and answering.

"Hey Blair, it's Ali. I was wondering if we could meet up at some point in the next day or so to go over some initial designs." Her voice sounded sultry through the speaker of her cell.

"Hi, Ali! Of course, are you free today? I could make it over during my lunch break," Blair answered, a smile creeping onto her face as she listened to Ali. She was excited to see what Ali had come up with. She was excited to see Ali, period.

"Great, well why don't we just make it a lunch date then, shall I meet you at Guido's?"

"Perfect, see you then." Blair hung up and reminded herself that this was work, not a date.

~***~

Paula stood silently in the doorway to Ali's office, listening to the conversation her boss was having. She wasn't intentionally eavesdropping, just waiting patiently to speak to her, but she saw the smile appear on her boss's face while she spoke into the handset, and then again as she listened to the person on the other end. She wondered if maybe Ali had hit a turning point in her life, one they all knew Susan would approve of.

"A lunch date, huh? Finally making good on that promise." The secretary smiled as she spoke, glancing quickly at the copy of Susan's letter on the wall.

"I'm meeting Blair. It's a working lunch, that's all. I don't recall there being a time limit on the promise," she said a little abruptly, and Paula grimaced.

"Uh sorry, yeah, I—"

"I know what everyone thinks, Paula. I know everyone has read Susan's letter, and you all want what is apparently best for me, but meeting someone else right now, dating again? No, I am not ready for that. I am not sure I ever will be, to be honest." She stood and moved across the room to place a file in its drawer, pulling a different one out and walking back to her desk. "Blair is a friend, someone that understands what I have gone through, that's all." Just because a beautiful woman had come into her life, didn't mean that Ali had to fawn all over her, did it?

"Yes boss, I'm sorry Ali." And she meant it; she hadn't wanted to cause Ali any hurt or embarrassment.

"If you could make sure I am not disturbed for the next hour, I would appreciate it." She sat back in her chair and contemplated her thoughts. Blair was beautiful; she hadn't noticed that before. When she was living with them, Ali had to shamefully admit that she had never really given Blair much of an appraisal as anyone more than a capable nurse. A friendship of such had developed naturally, but she had never looked at Blair as an available woman. She shook herself. She wasn't going to start now either.

Chapter Eight


Guido's was a fancy little Italian restaurant in the heart of the city. Situated alongside other eateries, it stood out mainly because it was painted in the colours of the Italian national flag, and every table inside and out was generally busy. Its reputation for quality food served at reasonable prices meant that Guido's never had an empty seat for long.

Ali had booked in advance, and as it was a nice day, she had requested an outside table. It was always nice to dine al fresco, Susan had told her. It was what the Europeans did. She watched a couple sitting not too far from her, talking animatedly as their hands reached for each other. She couldn't help the sharp prick of jealousy as he leant in to kiss his lover's cheek. She would be grateful when Blair arrived and she wouldn't have time to sit and dwell on what she had lost.

A taxi pulled up along the kerbside, and the blonde climbed out of the back seat. She bent slightly to pay the driver through the window of his door. She was tall, like Ali, and she wore her hair swept back into a compliant ponytail much like Ali's was during office hours. She was wearing an elegant navy-blue skirt and matching jacket this time that was complemented by an ivory-coloured blouse. Her heels, although not too high, only accentuated her calves. She was, Ali thought, a beautiful woman. She wondered why she hadn't noticed that before. She wondered why nobody else had noticed that too. She wondered why it was that she kept noticing it now.

Blair smiled when she realised that Ali had beaten her to the restaurant, giving a small wave as she casually sauntered down the sidewalk to where Ali sat. The darker of the two stood, and they embraced with a smile and a squeeze of hands.

"Hi, I am so glad you picked an outside table. I have been stuck in a stuffy office all morning," Blair declared, her eyes shining with enthusiasm as usual. It was infectious, the way she was so passionate about everything. Just being in her presence seemed to lift Ali.

"Sometimes lunch is the only time I get to see the sun," Ali countered. "Take a seat, I ordered us some bread and olives while we decide what to have, though to be honest I already know it will be the king prawn linguine." She smiled at Blair, who picked up her menu to glance through.

*"Always predictable at Guido's!" Susan laughed.*

*"I like the prawns, what can I say?" She leant across the table and placed a soft kiss on the corner of her wife's mouth.*

*"You have whatever you want, gorgeous. I love you." Susan smiled her trademark grin and plucked an olive from the bowl, popping it into her mouth with a wink.*

The waiter appeared, wearing a clean, crisp white shirt with immaculate waistcoat and black trousers to match. His name was

Sergio, according to the small silver name badge pinned to his chest next to a tiny pin of Italy's flag.

"Good afternoon ladies, may I take your drink order?" he said, exhibiting politeness to a fault, his voice breaking Ali's thought pattern and bringing her back to the present. She had expected him to have an accent, but he sounded as homegrown as she was.

"Are we drinking or behaving?" Blair asked Ali. She received a grin as Ali checked her watch.

"Pinot Grigio?"

"One bottle of Pinot Grigio then please, Sergio." Blair spoke eloquently, a slight bounce of mischief in her pronunciation of the wine. There were times when Blair reminded Ali very much of Susan. She felt instantly at ease with Blair in the same way she had when she had first met Susan, but they were so different too. Susan would never have chased a dream the way that Blair was doing. Susan was comfortable with where she was in life, but she knew who she was just as Blair did. Susan, however, would not have agreed to drink alcohol at lunchtime when she knew Ali was supposed to get back to work afterwards. But Blair, she had that touch of daring about her, and it was something that Ali realised she needed right now. She gave herself a mental slap. Why was she comparing Blair with Susan anyway?

"Okay so, I came up with a few designs and ideas. Firstly, we have colour boards. I wanted to show you several options." She pulled her briefcase up onto her lap and began to pull folders out from it. "Of course, the colour scheme you ultimately choose might impact on the design you want, because the hues and shades, et cetera, might not come through and pop like they would with a different set, but anyway..." She finished speaking as she lay the different styles and boards out on the table for Blair to explore, aware that Blair was studying her.

"Wow, Ali? You came up with this in just a few days?" she gushed, just as Sergio reappeared with their bottle of wine and two glasses. He placed them on the table and poured a little into each glass once Ali acknowledged she didn't need to taste it first. He then retreated, with the promise to return in a few minutes to take their order.

"Well." Ali blushed a little. It wasn't that she wasn't used to compliments about her work, because she got them regularly, but because it was Blair, her friend. "Some are just a generic base from which to begin but, well to be honest Blair, you excite me." She noticed the blush that now appeared on the cheeks of the woman sitting in front of her and realised what she had just said. She laughed and clarified. "Your enthusiasm excited me! I came away from Promise Hills just enthused and I...I want to help. I want other people like Susan to benefit from all the plans you have in place."

Sergio appeared once more, pad in hand to take their orders. Ali went with the linguine and king prawns as was expected while Blair decided to try the lasagne, having heard a great review for it from Ali.

"So, now we have established that I excite you—" Blair said, with a grin that lit up her face and made Ali giggle, "I should add that I am really glad to be in contact with you again. My life has been quite transient, and keeping relationships with friends going smoothly has at times been...difficult. Not a lot of people understood why I had to take live-in jobs and care for strangers 24/7 rather than find an evening to have dinner with them, I think they took it personally and as such, I have very few people to call friends," she explained without a hint of sadness. She had made a choice, a choice between helping others in a time when she was able to give them the best they could want or enjoying her own life. She didn't feel bad about that, but she planned on changing it.

"I think what you do is admirable. There are not so many people that can do that, Blair. I would rather have a friend like you, who I saw little of but knew she was doing something inspirational, than bucket loads of pals who just want to get drunk."

"Thanks, it can be a lonely life, and obviously now I have more time...I don't have the friends to enjoy it with."

"Well, I don't understand why you're not inundated with offers," Ali said, an honest appraisal.

"Ok, ok, so we appreciate one another, shall we move on to other subjects now?" Blair laughed it off; she needed to steer this conversation in a different direction before she did or said something stupid and embarrassed herself and Ali.

"Alright, what do you want to talk about?" Ali acquiesced.

Blair chuckled. "Anything you like." She popped an olive into her mouth and stared at Ali, waiting for her to respond.

"Anything? Ya know, Susan would say that and live to regret it!" She realised in an instant what she had just said. Her eyes closed as she fought to contain the tears that were threatening to surface.

"Susan lived to regret nothing, Ali," Blair said. Reaching across the table, she placed her fingers gently upon Ali's arm. "She told me that she had done pretty much everything she wanted to do in life, everything she had a say in any way, and her biggest accomplishment was making you fall in love with her."

"She said that?"

Blair nodded. "We used to talk quite a bit about you, I was quite jealous!" She laughed at the admission. "She would watch you leave the room and then turn to me and say, 'Great ass, don't ya think?'" She blushed a little at the retelling but smiled along all the same.

"Yeah, she always did love my ass." Ali laughed, proud of that little fact.

"Yep, or she would say, 'When I am gone, someone else is going to be so lucky, don't you think?' and I would have to agree with her again."

"Oh, so you agreed I had a great ass?" Ali asked, mock shock apparent on her face before she grinned.

"Have, not had!" she countered with a smirk. "And yes, I checked you out, on Susan's behalf of course." She wouldn't admit that even now she was struggling not to check Ali out. She felt a little guilty. They weren't on a date; she had no right to be yearning after Ali when Ali had no idea how she was feeling, but that didn't make it any easier not to.

Their waiter appeared and just about saved Blair's blushes as he passed over two plates of steaming pasta. The smell of tomatoes and oregano wafted through the air.

"This was a great idea," Blair said once she had swallowed her first mouthful. "Maybe, we could do it again?" The offer a tentative but honest one. She wanted to do this again, with no illusions as to what it was.

Ali nodded as she chewed, savouring the flavours of the pasta. "Yes, why not? It would do us both good, don't ya think?"

"I think so. I know that I always enjoyed spending time with you."

"Well, you did make great coffee." Ali smiled. "More wine?" she asked, lifting the bottle from the cold bucket to the side of them. Blair nodded with a grin, and Ali topped her up. "And we should drink more wine, too."

"Absolutely," Blair said, holding her glass in the air. "Cheers."

"Cheers!" Ali raised her own glass and clinked it against Blair's, a pact.

Chapter Nine


For several days, Ali threw herself into nothing else but the Promise Hills project. She was completely immersed when at four p.m., her office door swung open and Blair strolled inside unannounced.

"You and I have a date with this bottle of wine and these!" she declared, holding out a box from the lovely little cake shop along the street in one hand and a bottle of chardonnay in the other. She was in jeans that hugged her figure like they were painted on and a sweatshirt that hung loosely off her left shoulder and over her hips. High tops finished the look. She was make-up free and looked refreshed and happy as she perched herself on the corner of Ali's desk.

"Oh, I didn't realise I had arranged to meet—" Ali looked at her watch as Blair laughed and jumped in.

"Nope, you didn't, but I have sent you four emails, and as you didn't answer any of them. I called and spoke to Paula who, after much avoidance and I might add a very protective statement of intent, informed me that you haven't taken a real break for four days!" She placed the bottle and the box of cakes down on the desk. "And that is just not acceptable, Ali. So, turn that computer off and get your coat."

Ali stared at her as though she had lost her mind. Firstly, nobody ever dared to enter her office unannounced, and secondly, they especially didn't come in ordering her around. And yet, she didn't really mind so much other than that she was just far too busy.

"I have a lot to get finished," she said, waving her hand across the paperwork on her desk. "I really have to—"

"Put your coat on, come on! Let's go!" Blair walked around the desk and pulled Ali's fitted black jacket from the hook in the wall and brought it around her shoulders, holding it in place until Ali succumbed and pushed her arms into the sleeves. As she stood there waiting, she noted the framed letter on the wall and recalled the beautiful words that Susan had left for Ali.

"Fine, okay but I just need to—" She reached across the desk and hit a few buttons on the keyboard. "Ok, I'm ready. Where are we going?"

"Well, I figured we could hang out at your place, and that way when you have finally relaxed, you can climb into bed and actually get some sleep." She placed her hands on the top of Ali's shoulders and gently pushed her around the desk, pausing only to pick up the cakes and wine.

~***~

Blair noted that nothing much had changed in the time since Susan had passed, not that she expected it to. There weren't many clients whose homes she returned to after the client had passed, but there had been a few, and in every case, they had all kept things pretty much as they were when the person they missed had been alive. It was as if by keeping everything the same, they somehow kept something of their loved one with them. She guessed it made sense in some way. She probably would have done the same after her mother died if she had had the chance, but being just 17 at the time, she had had no option but to move in with her aunt and give up the home that she had shared with her mother. With limited space, she had only been able to take essential things with her: her clothes and school books, a small box of photographs and letters, and her favourite bear that her mother had bought her for her fourth birthday, a bear that she still had to this day in her office, a reminder much like Ali's letter.

"So, you have kidnapped me from my office, where is the cake?" Ali smiled as she walked the short distance to the kitchen and pulled out two glasses and a couple of plates, lining them up neatly on the countertop.

Blair went to the drawer she knew she would find the corkscrew in and opened the bottle, and then she poured two glasses. She stood quietly and watched as Ali opened the cake box.

She was a little mesmerized as Ali's tongue slipped out and licked her upper lip. She then bit down on her lower lip as she considered which cake was most appealing. She hooked her hair behind her ear and then gently reached forward to pluck the cake she had finally decided upon from its place inside the box, placing it delicately on the plate before returning to the box and positioning the other cake onto the plate she had put out for Blair. She licked her fingers and then, having the feeling she was being watched, she slowly turned her head to see Blair standing, her back resting against the edge of the sink. She had her left arm wrapped around her waist, and in her right hand she held a glass of wine that she was sipping from, an eyebrow raised as she watched the cake choosing.

"Figured out what you want?" Blair smirked. She couldn't help the little hint of flirtation in her voice.

"Yes, the best one." Ali returned the smirk and picked up the plates to carry them through to the living room. "Always the best one."

Blair picked up Ali's glass and followed behind her, reminded once more of Susan's liking for Ali's backside.

They sank down into the couch, one at either end. Ali pulled her shoes off and dragged her feet up underneath her, and both took a bite of the delicious cakes they had, crumbs and cream threatening to drop everywhere.

"So, how's it going?" Blair inquired, the cushion comfortably collapsing behind her as she relaxed into the space she had called home for six months of her life.

"Well, I have all the designs back and will be ready to present them by the start of next week," Ali said in reply, her wine glass slowly emptying with each sip.

"That's great, but I was actually asking about you!"

"Oh." She looked up and found Blair watching her expectantly, brown eyes focused fully on Ali. "I'm good, yeah. You know, keeping busy and—" She had found a spot on the coffee table that was easier to stare at than Blair's kind eyes.

"And ignoring any semblance of life moving forward?"

Ali glanced at her once more. Blair's warm coffee eyes narrowed at her, so she looked away again.

"It isn't that I'm ignoring it, I just—" She brushed her fingers through her dark hair and grabbed a fistful before letting it all fall around her face again as her head rested on her palm, the plate teetering gently on her thigh. "I don't really know how. How am I supposed to move on?" She felt the sharp sting of salty tears appear and tried blinking them away.

"Do you think there is a rule book, Ali?" Blair said softly, leaning forward and placing her palm gently on Ali's knee. "There isn't, you just have to try and keep your mind open to new things."

"I do, I'm here with you, aren't I?" she chuckled.

"Ah well, yes you are, although I think I had to kidnap you, so I'm not quite so sure it counts!" She laughed and sat back in her seat, taking another bite of her pastry.

"What about you? Anything fun on the horizon?" Ali asked, changing the subject just a little.

x

x

"As a matter of fact, I went on a date just yesterday." She sat forward and picked up the bottle, pouring a little more into each glass.

"And? How did it go?"

"She's nice," Blair said, with little or no real interest. Josie was cute and fun, everything her dating profile said she would be, but...there was something missing.

"Nice?" Ali raised a brow. "Just nice?"

"Well no, she was really nice; lovely in fact but, I'm not feeling it," Blair divulged, feeling a need to explain.

"So, not seeing her again then?"

"Of course I am, she's fun and not looking for anything serious, and that suits me right now." She didn't feel bad for using Josie this way; it was a mutually agreed upon option. An option that gave her a bit of breathing space from thinking about Ali.

Ali took a moment to consider this information. There was a little bit of a pull in the depths of her stomach, and she wasn't sure why the thought of Blair dating and having fun bothered her. She supposed it was because it meant less time she would get with her friend. If she felt a little bit jealous then that was all it was: she was fearing a loss. Again.

"Why don't you join us?" Blair was saying, proud of herself for being so magnanimous. Maybe it would do Ali good to get out and meet someone new.

"No way, I am not being the third wheel on your date."

Blair laughed loudly as Ali pulled a face. "I wasn't planning that. Josie has a friend..." She felt a little less noble when she considered the fact that she didn't actually know any of Josie's friends. She just wanted Ali to go out with them, with her.

"No!" Ali stated firmly, cutting Blair off before she could even think about finishing that sentence. "I am not ready to date, Blair."

"It wouldn't be a date, it would just be four women going out for a meal, maybe some drinks, and then see where the night takes them," Blair said.

"That's a date!" Ali laughed, and Blair couldn't help but smile. She was caught!

"I will make sure that Josie knows you're not there for a date," she asserted, waiting for Ali to respond. It took a moment which, in Blair's opinion at least, meant that Ali was considering it, but eventually Ali shook her head.

"No, thank you, but I—" She paused and thought about her words, needing to be honest. "I just don't want to right now."

Blair nodded. She would push Ali, a little here, a little there, but she wouldn't force her. Moving forward had to be something that Ali wanted to do, even if she didn't know how.

"So, what about we do something you've never done before? Something you've always wanted to try!" Blair reconsidered.

"You don't have to babysit me, you know?" Ali said, a little put out that Blair thought she needed handling.

"Is that what you think I am doing? I thought we were friends, friends do things together, don't they?" Blair answered, observing how Ali instantly returned to her hard-ass routine whenever she felt a little uncomfortable. She also noted Ali immediately soften, her bristly exterior put back in its box, for now.

"Yes, sorry. Did you have anything in mind?"

"Not really, I figured you would have something you wanted to do," Blair offered. She picked up the bottle to top them up once more and grimaced at the lack of wine left. "Is it just me or do these bottles get smaller?"

"I think it might be that the glasses have gotten bigger." She untucked her feet and placed the glass and plate on the table. "There's another bottle in the fridge, I'm just going to get changed. This suit is fine for the office but—" She didn't finish the sentence; there was no need as Blair nodded her agreement.

~***~

Her room, their room as she still thought of it, was quiet, the stillness of the evening surrounding her like a heavy sigh. Her shoulders sagged as she shrugged off her jacket and began to unbutton her cotton blouse, the teal colour working well with her skin tone. Clad in just a bra and suit pants, she strolled across the plush carpet barefoot to the walk-in closet. She tossed the dirty shirt into the washing basket and pulled a clean t-shirt from the drawer. The light material felt snug against her skin as she pulled it down over her chest. Unbuckling her belt, flicking the button open and, dragging the zipper down, she pulled off her pants. It was then her eyes were drawn to the intricate wooden trunk in the corner that she had stored all of Susan's things in.

*"You know you should have a bucket list too,"* Susan *suggested as she sat at the kitchen table writing out her own list.*

*"Hmm, I think I have enough things to do already,"* Ali replied. *Walking up behind her wife, she leant down and wrapped her arms around her neck from behind, kissing the small patch of skin that was right there waiting for her lips to gently press against.*

*"It might be fun to write even if you never do it,"* she replied, *her own hands reaching up to hold the arms around her as she tilted her neck and made room for the gentle caress.*

*"Well, then what is the point of that?"* Ali chuckled against her *ear, sending shivers up and down her spine.*

Blair stood in the doorway watching Ali, who sat cross-legged on the floor of her closet, bare legs and clothed top in front of the wooden trunk, lost somewhere in a memory.

She had only come looking for her because she had been gone longer than the general time it took to get changed out of work clothes. Now as she saw the box, she knew why, and her heart melted at the sight.

"Ali?" she asked softly. She saw the dark hair in front of her shake itself as Ali came back from whatever recollection she was having. Her head whipped around to see Blair walking toward her.

"Hey, sorry I—" she started to explain as Blair bent down behind her and wrapped her arms around her the way Ali had done with Susan. Blair held her as she wept. "Everything I do just reminds me of her."

Chapter Ten

Ali Jenkins had made a promise, this time to Blair. A promise that they would spend the weekend writing out a bucket list that they would then begin to pick off. She had no clue how on earth Blair had managed to get her to make this promise, but that was exactly what she had done, and so Ali had no option but to go along with it. Maybe it had been the memory of Susan and her bucket list, or maybe it had been the second bottle of wine, but whatever it was, she was stuck with figuring out what to add to hers.

There was still an hour or so before Blair would arrive. They were going to have lunch, write the list, and then go and do one of the easier ones that evening. At least that was the plan!

While getting dressed, Ali once more noticed the box in the corner. She slowly crossed the closet and sat down next to it. The clasp of solid brass flipped open at her touch. Reaching in, she pulled the flimsy piece of paper from between two books that had kept it safe this past year or more. Susan's bucket list.

She read through them, simple things like:

*Go to the beach one last time.*

*Swim in the ocean.*

*Ride a horse.*

*Stay up all night looking at the stars.*

*Drive over 100mph.*

She remembered doing all of them with Susan, and more. Carrying her into the ocean because she was too weak to walk. Letting her drive the Audi along the highway at 100mph because if she got caught, she could knock getting a speeding ticket or being arrested off her list.

*"If you think hard enough, there are a ton of things you'll want to do,"* Susan whispered as they lay in the hammock at 2 a.m. *The night sky was clear as it could be, stars twinkling brightly above them.*

*"I have everything I want right here, right now,"* Ali had said in reply, *pulling the blanket up higher around them.*

*"I always thought you would want to do something a little wild,"* Susan continued, *ignoring the fact that Ali didn't want to come up with anything other than being with her; she wasn't going to be here.*

*"I could see you coming up with a million things I could do on this bucket list."* Ali chuckled. *"I'm not sure I'd want to do any of them! God knows what you'd have me doing."*

*"Kayaking!"*

*"Kayaking? Really?"* Ali had to laugh now, *"Where on Earth did that come from?"* She could feel Susan chuckling in front of her, *the gentle shake of her shoulders.*

*"Well something exciting anyway, paragliding?"*

*"No, feet on the ground for me, I think."*

The doorbell rang out loudly as Ali placed the precious piece of paper back in its place inside the beautiful box. She grabbed a jumper and pulled it on as she walked briskly to the stairs. Skipping down them almost two at a time, she reached the door and opened it just as Blair was reaching to press the doorbell again.

"Hey, sorry, I was just getting dressed," Ali said brightly, indicating her attire and noting that Blair had chosen something similar to wear, only she had shorter sleeves.

"No problem, it's beautiful out here anyway," Blair replied as she followed Ali inside the house. "Maybe we should sit in the garden and have lunch?"

"That sounds like a great idea," Ali answered. She began to pull a tray down and place all the plates, glasses, and cutlery on it. Blair noticed the pad and pen sitting on the countertop and couldn't help but wonder if there was anything on it yet.

"Here, let me take that," Blair said, taking the tray from Ali and walking toward the backyard. Ali studied her as she walked by. Blair looked very relaxed and, Ali thought, very at home here. It made her smile.

The sun was scorching outside. The garden looked parched, and Ali made a mental note to turn the sprinkler on later; the flowers would be grateful. They set their lunch up on the glass table: two plates, two cups, one jug of iced sweet tea. Ali had thrown together a salad and tossed in some roasted chicken to bulk it out. Blair had brought with her an artisan olive loaf. They poured olive oil, sprinkled vinegar, and drank some tea in a harmonious silence.

Ali pondered that. Usually, she felt the need to speak, to break the monotony of quietness. It often felt uncomfortable to her to sit with just one other person, not speaking, because generally, the only time she sat with people was in order to speak: work matters, interviews, meetings. When her friends or family came to visit it was to catch up, to speak loudly about the weeks previously or the latest gossip involving their single cousin. Not since Susan had Ali just sat comfortably in silence with another person. There she was again, comparing Blair with Susan, why did she keep doing that?

*"It's one of my most favourite things to do," Susan had stated out of nowhere.*

*"What is?" Ali had replied, shaken from her doze in the sunlight by the break in silence from Susan's words.*

*"This! Just sitting here, with you, not speaking. It's one of my favourite things, it isn't something you can do with just anyone."*

*"Yeah, it's nice," Ali had said, before drifting back off to sleep again.*

She was shaken from her memory once again. This time it was Blair speaking quietly to her.

"What are you thinking about over there?" she said, staring intently from across the table. Ali smiled and then chuckled to herself.

"I was just considering how much I enjoy just sitting, in silence."

Blair nodded as though she understood immediately. "Yeah, the world is so noisy, sometimes it's nice to just sit and be still."

"Indeed, it's just—" Ali pondered how to explain what she felt. "It isn't often that you can do it with someone else. I mean comfortably, without feeling the need to break the silence because it's awkward. I—" She paused again. "I don't feel awkward with you, Blair." She smiled now, a shy, small smile that brought with it a slight blush.

"That's good because I've made plans to be here all day!"

They finished lunch in relative silence, aside from the odd comment here and there about how good the salad was or where did the olive loaf come from? Ali was used to small talk about work lately. It was a safe subject, one that didn't make her cry, but Blair never once mentioned it, even though technically she was a client and the presentation was due on Monday. And Ali liked that. Quite simply, she liked lots of things about Blair, she realised.

She picked up her pen from on top of the notebook and then found the page inside that she had headlined 'Bucket list,' scribbling something down quickly before she forgot.

"Hey, you're starting without me!?" Blair exclaimed with a grin.

"No, well yes, but only because if I don't write it down now, then I'll forget it." She closed the book and placed the pen back on top as it was, then slid it across the table so she could continue to pick at the bowl of olives.

"You're not going to tell me?"

"No! Not until both of us have ten things on our lists."

"Ten? Who made you rule maker!?" Blair laughed and threw an olive at her. Ali caught it and popped it into her mouth, grinning widely.

"Did you not know? I am always the boss." She laughed, knowing full well the only boss in this house had been Susan.

Chapter Eleven

The sun was lower in the sky and had moved slowly over the garden to shine at a different angle, basking them both in bright, but somewhat cooler, sunshine. The pair of them had been hard at it for thirty minutes, each with her own notebook and pen and an imagination filled with ideas. There was an agreement that anything they put down on paper had to be realistic. Flying to the moon or creating time travel was probably not going to happen to them in their lifetime, although Blair argued that if one of them did invent time travel they could probably go forward or backwards in time and find some way to go to the moon. Not that Ali really understood wanting to fly to the moon; she wasn't that keen on aeroplanes as it was, so she had no plans to get on a rocket ship. And if it were possible to go back in time, then the last thing she would be considering was anything that didn't involve getting Susan to the hospital a lot sooner. If only they had found that lump earlier... She sighed and refocused her attention back to Blair.

"How many have you got so far?" Blair asked, her pen stuck between her teeth as she glanced across the table at Ali. Her dark-haired friend looked so pensive as she considered her thoughts.

"Hmm." She counted down her list. "Five."

"Five!" Blair screeched a little out of fear and excitement. "From the woman that said she didn't have a bucket list in her?" The chuckle that followed made Ali stop what she was doing and look up.

*"Always pretending you don't want to do something when really it's all you can think about." Susan chuckled, and as she passed by she let her right hand drift across Ali's shoulder.*

"What's up?" Blair asked, suddenly serious and concerned. Ali looked as though she had seen a ghost.

"Do you ever..." She breathed deeply, unsure if she could explain without sounding crazy, or maybe she was crazy, clinging to something that wasn't there anymore. "When you laughed it reminded me of something. Something Susan said to me, and then as she walked away she brushed my shoulder and I—" She closed her eyes and faced the sky as she took a breath. "I felt it, just then I, I felt her touch my shoulder." She raised her own hand and touched the place where she had felt Susan.

Blair was unsure what to say. She had heard on many occasions from grieving people that they felt their loved one around them. Whether it was true or not she didn't know; she had never felt that way with her own mother. Once she was gone, she was gone, and it was only her memories that had kept her mother alive. When she thought a little more, she was sad about that. What if other people really did feel their loved ones around them still? Why hadn't her mother made it known that she was still around? Or maybe she had, and Blair just wasn't open to it. Either way, it saddened her to think she could be missing out.

"Maybe..." she began, but then changed tack. "Do you find comfort in believing you felt Susan?"

"Yes, but—" Her eyes misted. That haunted look that had been missing these past few days was back again. "How? How can she be here and not *be* here? How is that fair?"

"I don't know Ali, maybe when we die there is some part of us that lingers. An essence of us that stays with our loved ones." Blair stood and moved to the chair that had sat empty between them, putting her within arm's reach of her friend.

"I miss her Blair, I miss her so, so much," she wept, and Blair didn't waste a beat before she was there enclosing her in her arms and holding her tight. This beautiful woman who for so long had held everything in, trying to cope with the loss and devastation that death had brought to her life in an unwelcome gift wrapped in pain and hurt, now needed to release it all.

"I know sweetheart, I know." And she did know. She understood every tear, every whimper, and all the pain. And she also understood that wishful thinking wouldn't be enough; Ali was never going to look at her the way she looked at Susan.

When the sobbing had finally subsided, Blair reached back across the table and passed Ali a napkin. She blew her nose and wiped her eyes before laughing gently.

"God, you must wonder what you got yourself into?"

"Actually, I kinda like that you feel you can grieve with me," Blair returned. It took a certain level of intimacy to be able to let your feelings out the way Ali needed to; to do it with someone else present was a big thing. Most people did it by themselves, behind closed doors and away from the prying, pitying eyes.

"Is that what this is? It isn't like I didn't cry at the time," Ali said, running her fingers through her dark locks as she composed herself a little more. "Or like I haven't cried pretty much every time I've seen you." She laughed nervously.

"Most people will cry at the death, at the funeral, and even for a few days or weeks afterwards. But it isn't until months later that the reality sets in, that one finally understands that the relationship is, for want of a better word, dead." Blair spoke gently but firmly. She wanted Ali to understand her feelings were real, warranted, and to be expressed, but she also worried that Ali was holding on, clinging to any lifeline that kept Susan here in the present.

Blair took Ali's hands in her own, squeezing them gently as she brushed her thumbs over the back of her hands rhythmically before speaking once more.

"How about we open a bottle of wine and go through the items we've already come up with, and if you want to talk about Susan, then that's what we will do."

"Yes, that would be nice." She smiled sadly.

~***~

Bottle open and drinks poured, both women picked up their glasses and clinked them together. "To bucket lists and moving forward," Blair said, the smile on her face genuine. Regardless of how she felt about Ali, she would do anything to help her friend move forward.

"To bucket lists and moving forward," Ali agreed, though it took a little more effort for her to force out than it had for Blair.

"All right, I'll read my first line, then you, okay?" Blair offered, taking the initiative. When Ali nodded, she continued. "Okay, so my first item is—" She blushed a little and laughed with the embarrassment. "I want to visit a nudist beach." She watched as Ali's eyes widened and her mouth gaped.

"A nudist beach? As in we both have to get naked, on a beach?" Blair nodded, grinning at Ali's face and the shocked look that now adorned it.

"Well, I don't know if you have to get completely naked, or naked at all, but, yeah I want to try it. Don't you think it would be kinda freeing to be at one with nature like that?"

"With nature and however many other naked people?" Ali gasped. "Oh, I'm not so sure I could do that, Blair." Ali laughed then. *"You've never been shy before Ali."* Susan's voice echoed in her mind. She wasn't shy, so why was she so reticent about it?

"Okay, we can talk about it later, what's the first thing on your list?" Blair encouraged her.

"Well, it isn't as crazy as yours!" She started off light-hearted and smiling. "I want to send a message in a bottle."

"Okay, that we can definitely do, what will it say?" Blair asked.

"Well, I don't know yet, but something with my name and an email address maybe so whoever finds it can reply. I just thought it might be fun to see how far it goes." She felt embarrassed to admit such a simple thing. A childish thing really, but it was the first thing she had thought of.

"I think that would be great fun," Blair said as she reached out a reassuring hand that gripped Ali's arm and squeezed.

"Really? You don't think it's a little..." She paused. "Immature?"

"Hey, there is nothing wrong with being immature!" Blair laughed. "I plan to be immature quite often!"

"What else you got?" Ali said, laughing along with her.

"Fly a plane?" Blair suggested, unsure if it would be vetoed along with her fly to the moon idea.

"Alright, not something I look forward to either, but alright," Ali said, gritting her teeth. She hadn't actually considered how different Blair and she could be when it came to this. She had definitely underestimated that whole daring side of Blair.

"It will be great, imagine being up there in the clouds and having control of the machine as it glides through the air at high speed." Blair's arms moved through the air like wings as she imagined the freedom flying would give her.

"I—" Ali took a breath. It was time to woman up and start broadening her horizons. "You're just going to drag me out of every comfort zone I have, aren't you?" she laughed.

"You don't like flying?" Blair looked at her, eyes wide.

"Not really, I prefer to drive."

"Okay, then yep I am taking you flying out of your comfort zone!" Blair announced with a flourish, swallowing down the last drop of wine. She picked up the bottle and shared the remainder of the liquid between them both. "So, flying planes, nudist beaches, and a message in a bottle! What else ya got?"

"Alright, you can have your flying lesson and I'll raise you..." She locked eyes with her friend now, confidence surging through her as she brought out the biggest gun so far. "...one tattoo. And," she added quickly, "it has to be bigger than a dime!" She laughed, the look of fear on Blair's face evident. "What's up? Scared of needles?" she teased the nurse.

"Uh actually, yeah!" she admitted.

"What? You're a nurse, you stick people with needles all day long!" Ali exclaimed. This was something she had not expected.

"Yeah!" She laughed once more. "I can stick one in someone else, but sticking one in me? Like a thousand times a second? Oh no!" Blair was shaking her head as Ali stood to retrieve another bottle of wine. She held it up and waited for Blair to acknowledge that they were opening another.

"Oh yes, if I am getting naked, you are getting a tattoo." She walked away, a small spring in her step as she did so. Blair continued to watch her go before she spoke out loud and looked at the sky.

"Yeah Susan, she has got a great ass." And if she hadn't known any better, she could have sworn she heard a chuckle.

Chapter Twelve

"And so, Jenkins Graphics would like to thank you all for listening, and we hope that we have managed to work our magic and create the image that Promise Hills so richly deserves." Ali stood at the end of the conference room surrounded by easels that held the images she had come up with as part of the design structure for Blair. As she came to the end of her monologue, her fingers twisting her wedding ring around her finger was the only sign of any nervousness.

Her stomach, though, was doing somersaults, not a feeling she was used to having. Usually at a presentation she was supremely confident in her and her team's abilities but right now, with Blair and her backers all facing her, listening and watching intently as she presented the different colour schemes and ideas on how to present Promise Hills to its future patients, she felt as nervous as she had ever been.

*"You'll be fine Ali," Susan whispered. "It's just us."*

*"I know, I just – I want this so much, Susan." She found herself lost in the most beautiful green staring so adoringly back at her.*

*"So, let's go and get married then." She felt her hands being pulled as Susan led them toward the courthouse. Her smile was all Ali needed to see to bring her a calmness that sifted through her soul and evaporated every ounce of nerves.*

The room erupted into a round of applause. There were heads nodding and mouths smiling at her. She hadn't realised she had been holding her breath until Blair was standing in front of her, smiling. And as before with Susan, she felt the calmness swarming her cells.

"Wow, Ali, I cannot thank you enough for what you have done for us." Blair caught her by surprise when she leant in and kissed her cheek. Their hands had linked, and Ali found herself enjoying the feeling. Physical contact with someone had become the one thing she missed most. With Susan they were constantly touching one another, holding hands or touching delicately as they passed by one another. A hug while the kettle boiled, she missed that.

"I am so pleased that you liked it." Ali grinned, her tummy finally settled as she stood next to Blair, their hands still linked as one by one the Promise Hills committee members approached to offer congratulations to both women for all their hard work.

Jack, Sara, and Ola were working the room, explaining minor parts or more intricate designs details to those interested enough to ask. Champagne glasses clinked and laughter erupted through the babbling of voices.

"Everything we asked for and more Ali, thank you." Blair spoke sincerely as she held her friend's gaze. It was important to her that she knew and understood just how appreciated she was.

"You're welcome, Blair." The grin on her face was spreading, her eyes sparkled, and she looked as though something had lifted slightly from her shoulders.

"You look amazing too, Ali," Blair said, leaning in so nobody else could hear their conversation. "If nobody else has told you so, then I will." She winked and then thanked Fi as she passed by offering a glass of champagne from a tray she was carrying.

"Thank you, I have to say I did make an effort this morning, so it is nice that someone noticed," Ali said, taking a glass herself and sipping from it, still holding hands with Blair. She felt a warmth settle within her.

"Well, I think it's a shocking state of affairs that nobody has had the decency to tell you how great you look," Blair said again, unable to tear her eyes away. It was as though the room around them just melted away and all that existed in the world was Ali. Her heart thumped, and in her fantasy, this was the moment when she would lean in and kiss Ali, taste her on her lips. Somewhere in the distance, someone dropped a glass and the shattering sound brought them instantly back to the room. "I'm sorry, I didn't mean to embarrass you."

Ali shook her head. "You didn't, honestly its fine, I just...it's just been a long time ya know...since anyone..."

"Sure, I know." Blair smiled shyly and looked away.

Chapter Thirteen

The rest of the week went rather slowly for Ali. With her end of the project complete, she was back to the paperwork and organising that had become her area to deal with over the months since Susan's passing. Time dragged. Everything had been sent to printers and sign makers, and until it was all ready to be installed, she had little more than a few client meetings and briefings to attend to.

And for Blair, it was the complete opposite, which compounded Ali's boredom because she didn't even have the opportunity to sit down and catch up with her friend.

Blair had a lot going on at the hospice. It was just weeks away now from opening with its first patients, and she was bogged down in paperwork and last-minute interviews.

"I will be pleased once we have all the staff picked and ready to go," Blair said. The panel had taken a break from interviews, and she was enjoying a few minutes with Davina Garcia. It was Davina's mother who had employed the services of Blair after Susan and had given them both the opportunity to discuss the idea for the hospice. Davina had inherited a lot of money and was only too happy to be involved in this dream of Blair's.

"Yes, it will be almost the last puzzle piece in place."

"And then the signage should be in place by the end of the month and we're good to go." Blair was excited, but also a little daunted. There was so much to do, and she had felt the stress of it all over the last few months building.

"Ah yes, Ali has done a wonderful job." Davina turned to refill her cup as she continued to speak. "You make a stunning couple, I must say." She took Blair's cup and filled that also before handing it back to her.

"Oh, we're not...I mean Ali and I, we're not a couple." Blair blushed as she spat the words out quickly.

"Really? But you seem so...close."

"Yes, I met Ali a year ago when I nursed her wife," she explained, taking the offered cup. "Thank you."

"Well, I guess my instincts are off then, I thought she was your latest love interest." She giggled and leant in conspiratorially. "Maybe you should ask her." Davina left Blair with no opportunity to comment as she caught the attention of David Spencer, the other member of their three-person interview panel, and crossed the room to join him back at their table. The next interviewee was due any moment.

Blair had wanted to inform Davina how wrong she was, but she couldn't ignore her growing feelings, feelings that she had had for such a long time now.

Back then her thoughts and feelings would have been deemed inappropriate, which was why she had kept her distance this past year and more. Susan had known, of course; she had seen right away the way Blair had looked at Ali. She encouraged it too, to a certain degree, constantly making comments that meant Blair would have to look at Ali and agree with her. At the time she had laughed it off as Susan having a bit of fun, teasing her a little, but as the months passed and as Ali became more accepting of Blair in the home, Blair couldn't stop herself from falling a little bit in love with her.

She had watched the way Ali was with Susan, so full of love and admiration, never too busy or too tired to deal with anything Susan needed of her. Blair had rarely had anyone in her life who had given so much of themselves to make sure she was content, and there was Ali, in the last months of her wife's young life, giving her everything. She was gentle, and yet she had a fire inside her that burned so intensely at times that Blair thought she would scorch just from one of Ali's glares. When she had watched the way Ali would embrace Susan, her arms and legs wrapped around her protectively, she would feel the burn of jealousy – just for a second or two, but it was there.

When Susan passed, Blair knew nothing could come of her feelings, no matter what Susan had thought. Ali would never look at anyone the way she looked at Susan; that much was clear. As time passed and Blair found herself wrapped up in other clients and enjoying the odd date here and there, she thought less and less of her. That was, until her company needed a designer, and the first thought in her head was of the dark-haired, brooding, and gorgeous Ali Jenkins.

Now though, they were friends. There was a line that was drawn, and she was comfortable with that. She could honestly say she was happy just being friends with Ali, but that didn't mean she couldn't acknowledge her attraction to the woman.

They had plans to spend some time together over the weekend to do something on their bucket lists. There had been no decision yet as to which item they would choose. They would decide that over a bottle of wine and dinner on Friday night. But right now, she would enjoy her date with Josie and let all romantic notions of Ali Jenkins fall by the wayside as she indulged in an evening of raw lust – if she was lucky.

Chapter Fourteen

The night air that Friday was warm, and both Ali and Blair were contentedly lounging in the living room in comfortable clothing and no footwear. A box of half-eaten pizza and a bottle of Chardonnay sat just as easily on the table in front of them. Creedence Clearwater was playing on the stereo – something about a calm before the storm and had you ever seen the rain on a sunny day. It was from before Blair's time, but she listened with half an ear. Their notebooks were open, and both feverishly tried to work out the order in which they planned to accomplish the items on their list, the first of which would be completed the next day. Apparently.

As they continued with the task in hand, Blair had a text message come through on her phone. She looked at the screen that illuminated the first few words, reading them from where she sat without picking it up, and Ali noticed a small grin appear on her face.

"You can answer it, you know," Ali said, looking up from her pad to her friend. Blair sat slouched lazily in track pants, looking for all the world as though she belonged here, and that thought struck Ali as both horrid and wonderful at the same time.

She watched as Blair leant forward and picked up her phone. Swiping the screen, she quickly read the message again, grinned a little wider, and then hurriedly typed a reply before placing it back on the table.

"So, who is she?" Ali asked, grinning too. It was clearly a woman that had put that smile on Blair's face.

"Just Josie," Blair replied, not quite sounding as excited as she had looked.

"Just nice Josie?" Ali teased with a grin that made Blair giggle. The wine had definitely loosened her up.

"Yeah," Blair laughed. "Very nice Josie." Ali tried to smile at the admission, but something about it felt unsettling.

"So, how's that going?" She couldn't shake the small tug of irritation as she asked, which was unfair, and so she tucked it back away because that was not an appropriate response to your friend finding someone who potentially made her happy, just because you didn't want to lose the time you had with your friend. Because that was all it was, all it could be.

"Actually, surprisingly well. I didn't think it would go anywhere, we're so very different, but..." She looked at her friend, placing her notebook down in her lap. "I think maybe..."

"Wow, that's great Blair. I'm happy for you," Ali replied graciously. She swiftly turned away, forcing herself to stare at the page in her notebook instead. An overwhelming flush of jealousy suddenly made itself known. And this time she couldn't ignore it or pretend it was anything but what it was.

"I was hoping maybe you would like to meet her, ya know have dinner with us or..."

"Nope. Not being the third wheel, remember?" Ali said, refusing to look up from her notepad and look at her friend. The need to quash this jealousy was more evident than it had ever been before. She wasn't used to this feeling; it confused her, and she needed to push it away.

"Oh, okay well..." Blair didn't quite know what had upset Ali, but something clearly had, so changing the subject looked like the brightest thing to do. "Did you work out what you wanted to do first?"

"Hmm?" Ali answered. Her mind was elsewhere, still wandering the pathways of Blair and Josie. She shook herself mentally and desperately pushed those thoughts from her mind, concentrating only on Blair's words. Whatever this was, she would have to deal with it another time.

"The bucket list? Did you decide which one?"

"Oh, yeah I thought the message in a bottle would be easy enough." Finally, she looked toward Blair, who was smiling, a smile that said mischief. "What?"

"That requires going to the beach, doesn't it?" The grin on Blair's face was growing. So was the nervous feeling of excitement building within Ali.

"Yes," Ali answered slowly, nervously! "Why?" The nerves now far exceeding the excitement.

"Well, I did some investigating, and we're out of luck on the nudist beach thing," Blair confirmed, noting the relieved reaction spreading across Ali's face.

"Oh, that's an awful shame." Ali grinned, tucking her feet up beneath her as she got more comfortable, all thoughts of Blair's love life out of her mind.

"Ah but, see I also added another thing, which according to our agreement, you have to do too." There was a twinkle in Blair's eye that instantly brought the nervous apprehension back to Ali.

"Uh huh," said Ali, her eyes widening even more. This daring side of Blair was so very captivating.

"So, I added break the law!"

"Break the – are you crazy?" Ali laughed. For the first time in a long while, she really laughed.

Blair was laughing too. "Yes! We go to the beach, skinny dip, and then throw in our bottles, and that will be three things we can cross straight off the list." For Blair, it really was that simple, and she had a feeling that although Ali would protest everything to begin with, there was a part of her that wanted to be pushed out of her comfort zone.

Ali sat quietly, considering the plan in depth. She was a lip-biter, Blair decided. Whenever she had something to think about, she would bite her bottom lip. It was cute, sexy. She mentally slapped herself for thinking that way about her friend, but it was true.

"What are you doing Sunday?" When Ali spoke, she sounded quiet and a little unsure.

"Uh..." Blair glanced quickly at her phone. "Nothing yet."

"You have plans, it's fine. We can do it another time." Ali stood as she spoke and began to clear the pizza box, not because it needed to be cleared, but because she suddenly needed to be doing something, anything that didn't involve thinking of Blair out with someone else.

"Ali? I don't have any plans," Blair called out as she scrambled off the couch and followed Ali to the kitchen. She hadn't agreed to anything with Josie yet.

"Blair, please if you have a date with Josie that's fine, you don't need to lie to me to make me feel better," Ali said, moving clean pots from the draining board and placing them in the cupboards with a bang. She was angry and she had no right to be. She was jealous and she had no right to be. She didn't even understand *why* she was jealous.

"What? Ali? Why would I need to lie to you? I don't understand...feel better? About what?" Blair was confused about where this was heading. "Have I somehow upset you?" Ali stood motionless at the sink, her hands flat upon the surface as she fought to control the sudden emotional turmoil she was feeling.

"No, of course not, it's just me. I'm sorry." There was a moment, a simple bout of seconds when Blair made a decision. She closed the distance between them and placed her palms gently on Ali's shoulders, bringing their bodies closer together.

"Talk to me, Ali. What's going on?" The words were soft and quiet against her ear. No judgement; just a simple question, one that Ali didn't really have an answer for.

Ali turned in the space, but Blair didn't pull back. Instead, she placed a warm palm upon Ali's cheek and cupped it gently, her thumb wiping away the stray tear that edged its way downward.

"I'm here for you Ali," she whispered, bending slightly to look Ali in the eye. Her chin began to wobble, and Blair pulled her close against her.

"I just miss..." Blair waited for the name Susan to pass Ali's lips, but instead, she surprised her. "This. I miss this." She just needed to be held, Blair realised as she allowed her friend to sob against her chest.

"Oh, sweetheart." Blair wrapped her arms fully around her and held tight until she felt Ali begin to relax. She felt her heart melt. Every feeling she ever had for this woman she had pushed away and ignored, and yet now, here with Ali clinging to her, it all came flooding back in and she didn't know what to do with it, or how to deal with it.

Ali pulled back and stared at her. The way in which Ali held her gaze was intense and penetrating. They were so close, breathing each other in with stuttering breaths. All she had to do was lean in and they would be kissing, and she wasn't sure anymore if Ali would stop her. She could feel Ali's fingers tightening and loosening their grip on her shirt, the movement sending a tremor down Blair's spine. She just had to lean in, capture those lips with her own. She cleared her throat, swallowing once as she pushed it all back down again.

"Hey, why don't I get some hot chocolate made while you go clean up," she whispered instead, "and then we can sit on the couch and watch a crappy movie, and if you want me to hold you then that's just fine." She placed a small kiss on Ali's forehead, her lips lingering for a just a second longer than she needed them to. Ali smiled and nodded in agreement.

"Ok." Ali wiped her face on her sleeve. Squeezing Blair's arm, she left the room. With Ali gone, Blair took a deep breath and made an attempt to get a grip of herself.

~***~

Ali stood at the top of the stairs and held the bannister tightly in her grip. What had just happened? She could feel her head swarming with thoughts and feelings that she didn't know what to do with. It made her feel giddy. Staring into Blair's eyes, she had seen something, something that she couldn't quite get a hold of. And she couldn't stop herself, couldn't tear her eyes away. It was only Blair closing them that had broken the connection and brought normality back into the room. She closed her own eyes and was instantly transported back into Blair's arms, where she felt safe and loved. She felt loved, that's what she had seen. That was what she couldn't tear her eyes away from.

Chapter Fifteen

Confusion. Ali stirred slightly, her brain foggy with sleep still. She felt warm and yet she ached. She tried to move and found herself trapped in a confined space. Then she heard it: a small groan. Then she felt it: fingers gripping her a little bit tighter. For the briefest moment, she thought of Susan tucked up tight against her, but then she remembered being upset and curling up on the sofa to watch a movie, with Blair.

She lay there silently and considered how she felt about it. It was kind of nice. It was the one thing she missed most since losing Susan: just being in the arms of someone, but not just anyone. It wasn't Susan though, and that made the entire situation just wrong. Didn't it?

She was the little spoon right now, but with Susan, she had always been the big spoon. Her head was resting comfortably on a cushion with Blair's arm supporting her neck, and Blair's other arm was slung casually around her waist, her fingers splayed across her abdomen. She felt safe and happy, loved. She also felt terrified, and so she had to move.

~***~

The house was quiet, just the gentle sounds of contentment coming from Blair as she continued to sleep on the couch. Ali stood in the kitchen, leaning back against the sink watching her. It hadn't gone unnoticed that this was the same position she had been in last night, only this time she was calm and in control. And Blair wasn't staring back at her.

She had had time now to digest it. She was just going to take it for what it was, just a moment between two people who had been involved in a traumatic experience together.

She flicked the kettle on and pulled two mugs from the cupboard. It was no use; she couldn't shake it. She placed her hands down on the countertop and steadied herself, taking several deep, cleansing breaths. Steam from the kettle filled the space in front of her, and she flinched at the sound of the switch clicking off, breaking the silence. One question burned her: if it weren't for Susan, would she be attracted to Blair? No matter which way she asked herself, she only ever came to one conclusion.

"Coffee is ready, sleepyhead." Ali bent down by the couch and stroked Blair's hair as she gently woke her from her slumber. The mug of milky brown coffee was hot and steaming in her hand. Blair's nose twitched as the aroma made its way into her dream and brought her back to wakefulness.

"Hmm, morning. What time is it?" Blair mumbled, enjoying the moment of tenderness. It wasn't that often that she woke to fingers gently tugging through her hair.

"Nine," Ali said, glancing once again at her watch.

"You should have woken me." There was a sleepy smile on Blair's face. It reminded Ali of all those mornings the pair of them would share over coffee while Susan rested.

"Why? You looked comfy, so I figured I'd let you sleep. Anyway, coffee is ready, and breakfast won't be far behind." Grinning, Ali turned and left Blair to wake up. "Unless, I mean have you got to be somewhere?"

"No, you can have me." She blushed profusely as she realised what she had said, and surprisingly, Ali blushed too, the previous evening weighing heavily on both women's minds.

After the moment they had shared, it was surprisingly not awkward. They had snuggled on the sofa just like Blair had suggested; she had held Ali in her arms, and as she had fallen asleep, Blair had observed her. The deep frown of sadness had lifted as her features relaxed. When Ali had whimpered in her sleep and wriggled in closer to Blair, it had been torture, and it had taken all of Blair's restraint to stop herself from soothing her, kissing her.

~***~

"Ok, I need to get changed and showered, but then I'm going to come back here and pick you up," Blair said, wiping toast crumbs from her fingers. Breakfast had been nice. Both of them seemed to be happy with the idea of not talking about what had happened. It didn't stop the quick glances and shy smiles between conversation, but that seemed to be okay for now.

"And we're going to…"

"Go to the beach, of course."

"But, don't we have to buy a special bottle for our messages?" Ali asked, grabbing the chance to get out of this skinny-dipping idea. It was one thing to write it down on a bucket list, but to actually contemplate doing it, was quite another. Especially now.

"In case you haven't noticed, we have two wine bottles with perfectly good corks that will work. We can wrap our notes in those little lunch bags you have so many of, pop them in, and hey presto, we are ready to go." Blair raised her eyebrows and smiled a smile that said, 'you won't get out of this so easily.'

"Damn," Ali said, laughing. "You really are that desperate to see me naked, aren't you?"

"Well, I am pretty sure there are a lot of people who wouldn't be offended by it." She turned away quickly. There was that slight blush again; she could feel her cheeks burning, and she hoped to God that Ali didn't notice.

Ali had never been a prude. School locker rooms had been part of her teenage life, and she was accustomed to undressing and showering with other women, but that was then, and for the past 12 or so years, the only person who had seen her naked had been Susan. It was nerve-wracking now to consider being naked in front of anyone else. She closed her eyes, and when they opened again, she saw the letter from Susan on the wall. She knew it off by heart. '*Try new things.*'

"OK fine! Let's go get naked with nature."

Blair whooped and fist-punched the air. "Ha ok, yes I am an adult." She laughed as Ali raised an eyebrow at her friend's jubilant antics. "Get ready, I'll be back in an hour." And then she was gone.

The house was silent as Ali reached out and touched the framed letter. She swallowed hard and found herself on the brink of tears as she considered a tiny thought that had been pushing at her consciousness for a few days.

*"Let someone else in Ali, let someone else love you."*

*"What if I can't?" Ali had argued.*

*"But what if you can?" Susan had encouraged as she kissed her wife's soft lips and whispered, "What if you can?"*

"What if I can?" she said aloud before shaking herself and heading to her room to get ready.

Chapter Sixteen

A beach in the height of summer would normally be packed with vacationers, tourists, and children, but the beach that Blair had driven them to was deserted. It took them a couple of hours to drive out, and then once they had parked and grabbed their bags from the car, they had to take a short hike through a wooded area. It wasn't quite a forest, but the density of the evergreens blocked the sun from shining through in anything more than laser-like beams that penetrated like a colander on the green carpet beneath their feet. Once they cleared the trees, it was a steep climb down a short cliff to the hidden cove.

Ali was grateful that Blair had managed to find somewhere a little bit out of the way. With no nudist beaches for miles and miles and laws that frowned upon nudity, it had concerned Ali that they might actually get arrested, and that wasn't something she planned on doing soon, regardless of how 'fun' their bucket list ideas might be.

It was a warm day at least, and both women were perspiring with the exertion of the walk and climb.

Blair threw her bag down on the sand and stood to look out to sea while Ali kicked her shoes off and let the sand sink between her toes. The last time she had been at the beach had been when they had taken Susan, and she realised just how much she had missed it too. Her life had closed down with Susan's death. Things she used to enjoy doing all reminded her too much of being with Susan, and that would just make her upset, so she avoided anything that would cause that numbness that had settled so easily within her all those months ago.

While Blair unpacked and pulled out a blanket, Ali strolled down to the water's edge and let the ocean wash across her toes. Her thoughts drifted to dunking Susan under the water; she could still hear the shrieking that came as she submerged herself and Susan in the water. It hadn't been as cold as she had expected, and that was the same today. The water was warm on the shore from the sunshine that beat down on it.

When Blair drew up her bucket list, she did so with Ali in mind. She had made a promise herself to Susan that one day she would find a way to help Ali move forward. At the time she wasn't even sure if she would be able to keep that promise, but now that she had the opportunity, she would try her best not to let Susan down.

"Blair, I know when I am gone that Ali will need you," Susan had said as Blair helped her to dress one morning.

"I thought we agreed that I would stay on for a while when that time comes?" Blair answered, lifting Susan's sleep top gently from her frail body.

*"Yes, that's not what I meant though. You like her, don't you?"* she asked as though she had just asked a friend if she liked cake. It was expectant.

*"Of course, Ali is a lovely woman, why wouldn't I like her?"* Blair had questioned as she pulled the bottoms off too and prepared to wash Susan.

*"You like her more than just a friend, I see it. It's ok, I want someone to look at her that way. I want—"*

*Blair stopped what she was doing and knelt in front of her now-naked client. "Susan, what are you saying?"*

*"I am saying that if you like her, if you could love her, then I give you my blessing. Give her time, let her grieve me, and then when the time is right for you both—"* She hadn't finished her sentence because Ali had called from downstairs, but she had made it clear on many other occasions what she thought.

*"I don't think Ali will feel that way, Susan,"* Blair had whispered, not daring to imagine anything else. She liked Ali; in another world, who knew, but right now it wasn't appropriate.

*"Then promise me that you will at least help her move forward, help her find that place she can be to let someone else love her. Promise me, Blair."* Susan had a way of making you want to do as she asked, and Blair found herself nodding along and agreeing.

*"I promise I will help her if she lets me."*

"Hey." She felt the warmth of a hand on her arm bringing her back to reality. "You ok? You kinda did what I do and zoned out." Ali smiled.

"Yes, I'm good." Blair returned the smile, her eyes warming as she focused on Ali in front of her. "Did you already write your message?"

"I did," she said, pulling a piece of paper from her pocket, already wrapped in a plastic covering. "I even packed the bottles. So I guess, nothing like the present I suppose for this law-breaking nakedness you're so intent on." Ali looked as nervous as Blair had ever seen her.

"We don't have to do this Ali, not if you really don't want to," Blair said, suddenly aware of exactly what she had suggested they do. At the time it had been about pushing Ali out of her comfort zone, making her try new things, daring her. But now, now she was here and taking her top off, Blair found herself stalling. She wanted to watch, wanted to see the body underneath that she thought about too often, if she was honest, since that last day they spent on the beach with Susan.

*"Doesn't she look hot in that bikini?" Susan said, having caught the look Blair had given Ali as she passed.*

*"Susan, you know you have to stop doing that," Blair laughed, but deep down she couldn't argue.*

*"What? We can't appreciate that gorgeousness on display?"* she had smiled, the mischief in her eyes dancing with delight as Blair narrowed her eyes at her.

*"Ok fine, yes she looks hot."* She shook her head as she laughed along with Susan.

"Come on, I am not going to do this on my own. Strip!" Ali demanded as Blair laughed nervously.

She pulled off her own top, and both women laughed out loud at the ridiculousness of what they were about to do. They snuck glances at each other as trousers were yanked down, leaving them in just their underwear.

"Ready?" Ali asked as she reached behind her to unclasp her bra. Blair nodded and did the same, then looked around quickly to check there was nobody else in view before they both removed their panties. Blair reached for Ali's hand and was elated when she took it, and then they ran screaming and whooping down towards the ocean shore, sand kicking up behind them as they hit the water and kept going until it was deep enough to just fall into.

There was laughter, the spontaneous sounds of fun erupting from deep within. Both women, blonde and dark, up to their necks in the ocean, laughing.

"Oh my God!" Ali screamed. "That was exhilarating." She threw her head back and soaked her hair in the cool water, letting her feet float upwards she lay flat out on top of the water. Her perky breasts peaked above the water, tight nipples topping milky flesh as Blair tried not to gawp. Her flat, toned stomach glistened under the water as the sun beat down on them. Blair did the only thing she could think of to stop herself from staring and joined her friend in floating on top of the water.

~***~

It turned out that Blair was an excellent fire maker. Once they had dried off and gotten themselves dressed again, they had spent a little while walking up and down the shore collecting pieces of driftwood and large rocks to build a fire.

They sat huddled next to each other as the sun dropped lower in the sky. Far out to sea, the colours changed from blues to greys and oranges, reds and purples. The light from the fire glowed and lit their faces warm and bright.

"So, are we going to read each other's messages, or just poke them in the bottle and toss them?" Blair asked as Ali read her message and folded it for the 5th time.

"You can read it if you want to," Ali answered, holding the folded paper out to her. She took it, gingerly.

"You sure?"

"Yeah, go for it." She watched as Blair unfolded the letter and began to read.

*I cherish you and what we had. Thank you for loving me, for the memories we made. Thank you for sharing your life with me, for showing me what love is. So that one day I might recognise it again.*

When Blair finished reading she remained silent for a beat; her message suddenly didn't seem all that worth tossing after reading Ali's. "Ali, that's beautiful, really it's...Susan would be so proud of you."

"You think so? I, I don't know where it came from to be honest," Ali admitted quietly.

"I think it came from the heart, and that's all that matters, though ya know now I'm going to have to rewrite mine and make it just as relevant." Blair laughed and nudged her shoulder against Ali.

"Show me." She held her hand out for the letter and waited patiently until Blair finally gave in and handed it over. "'If found please email?' Really, that's all you put?" Ali looked at her friend, unable to hold in the bubble of laughter that erupted.

"I know, I told you, right? Ok, okay gimme a piece of paper."

Ali passed her her notebook and pen. "Get writing and make it good!"

~***~

The ocean tide was on its way back out, pulling away from the shore with every roll. It was relaxing to just sit in front of the fire listening to the waves crash gently with a quick roar before rippling back out and crashing forth again.

"This is nice," Ali said, a giant marshmallow on the end of the stick she held into the fire. "Thank you for pushing me to do this."

189

She pulled out the stick and tested the gooeyness. Finding it perfect, she shoved the marshmallow between two crackers and watched eagerly as it oozed out from the sides.

"You're welcome," Blair replied, watching as Ali enjoyed the s'more and then noticing as she shivered slightly. "You cold? I can, ya know, if you like I can—" She rambled a little before finally getting it out. "Hold you if, ya know, you—"

"Actually," Ali started, turning to speak directly to Blair. "I was always the big spoon."

"You want to hold me?" Blair clarified. Ali nodded. "Oh, okay sure."

And so they sat, one behind the other, on the beach in front of the fire. With Ali's arms pressed around her, Blair relaxed back, letting out a deep sigh of contentment. In the darkness, Ali was able to just enjoy the feeling of someone in her arms, even just for a little while. Just for tonight, she could enjoy it for what it was: her friend helping her to move forward.

"This is nice," Ali said. "Thank you for making me do this."

Blair leant her head backwards and rested it against Ali's shoulder. "Anytime."

She felt Ali's arms tighten their grip, and just for a moment, she enjoyed the feeling of being held by her.

Chapter Seventeen

"*Obe ata din din!*" That was what Ola had called out rather loudly from the kitchen. Apparently, if anyone wanted some, then they were to venture to the communal staff room, whereupon Ola would be dishing out bowlfuls of *obe ata din din*.

"Ok, now you know I am always up for trying anything you cook, Ola," Jack was saying as he hovered around the bubbly woman while she stirred and tasted. "But what the hell is it?"

She laughed heartily at the question. It was always more fun to make them eat first and then tell them what it was, but after she had threatened Jack with bush rat one afternoon when he was being particularly annoying, they had all made sure to check first what exactly it was she was offering.

"Jack, now what do you think it is?" She looked him square in the face with a genuinely angelic gaze.

"Hmm, well it looks like a lumpy soup," he said, looking down into the pan. She gave him a look of disdain before kissing her teeth at him.

"I don't know why I bother feeding you all." Pouring a large ladle into a bowl, she winked at Paula.

"It's pepper stew," came a voice from the hallway. Ali had been passing on her way to her office and overheard the conversation. Ola clapped excitedly.

"I see some of you are learning!" Ola exclaimed as she handed out more bowls of delicious stew. Her colleagues were now more than eager to be fed.

~***~

Following Ali into the office, Paula couldn't help but feel as though she were intruding on something. Her boss had arrived at work after everyone else, which was a first for Ali. Over the last year, they had even had competitions between them as to how early Ali came into the office. And now she was smiling as she read a message on her phone.

The morning had been busy as hell with meetings and client calls keeping them both within the confines of their own offices, so now Paula intended to take a few minutes and catch up.

"Ola is going to be impressed you knew her stew."

Ali glanced over her shoulder out of the door to make sure nobody was within earshot. "Google!" she said, winking at her secretary, who stood open-mouthed with a grin on her face.

"I should have thought of that." She laughed out loud before continuing. "You're in a very good mood today. Good weekend, I take it?" Ali stopped what she was doing and turned to give her assistant her full attention.

"Actually, yes, I had a really nice time. Blair and I went to the beach."

"Oh, it was good weather for that," she replied, watching as Ali smiled at the memory. It had been a lot of fun in the end. "So, you and Blair?"

"Are friends," she insisted once more. "Just friends." Why had she felt the need to reiterate that point? She wasn't sure. Why did they all assume otherwise? She was pretty sure she hadn't done anything to give them the wrong impression.

"Well, it looks good on you, Ali," Paula said, squeezing her arm as she passed once more.

"What does?"

"Happiness." She smiled. "Now, do you want some Obe dabby ding dong?" They both laughed as Ali nodded and Paula shouted up the corridor for two more bowls of fabulous stew.

Chapter Eighteen

Music blasted from the stereo as Ali danced around the room. She had no idea who was singing, but the beat had gotten her foot tapping all the same, and before she knew it she was moving. Grabbing a cup from the cupboard, she shimmied across the room and hit the switch on the kettle just as the cymbal crashed. She then turned on the spot and moonwalked to the fridge, bending at the knees and twerking as she grabbed the milk carton and stood slowly, seductively rolling her hips before she hot-trotted back to the kettle and waited, her hips swaying back and forth as she poured water and then topped up her coffee with milk just in time for the song to end and the DJ to start talking.

*"I don't think I have seen you let loose like that since our wedding." Susan laughed as they headed off the dance floor to get a drink. A new gay bar had opened in town, and they had hit the dance floor within minutes of arriving there.*

*"Oh God, I am going to feel it in the morning, but I love getting jiggy wid it," she laughed, singing the chorus to the song that had just been playing. "But only with you." Her palms planted firmly upon Susan's chest, moving slowly up until she had a handful of her collar and she pulled her closer. "When you're dancing with me like that, I just want to take you home and—" She didn't get to finish the sentence before hot, wet lips covered hers,*

*pressing and pushing her mouth to open and accept the tongue that wanted to play.*

*"You need to let loose more often," Susan gasped, catching her breath as they clung to one another.*

The telephone ringing brought her out of her memory and back to the reality of her life. Alone.

"Hello?"

"Hey, it's me." Ali found herself feeling lighter as Blair continued to speak. "Are you busy? I had this idea, and I know how so very excited you are by me and my ideas." Ali could hear the humour in her voice and couldn't hide the smile it brought forth. She caught a glimpse of herself in the reflection of the window. Paula was right; happiness did look good on her.

"Hmm, do I actually want to know what idea you've come up with now?"

"Of course you do! Excited by me, remember? Your words, not mine." She laughed, not giving Ali a chance to respond as she continued. "Now, are you willing to spend one hour with me having fun?"

It was almost 7 p.m., but it was still light outside, the summer's sun particularly warm this week. She wasn't tired, but she hadn't eaten. Still, she really didn't have an excuse not to say yes, though, and if the truth be known, she didn't want to say anything but yes.

"Ok, doing what?"

"Firstly, what are you wearing?" Blair said the words seductively as though they were about to engage in something completely different to what Ali expected, but then Blair laughed, and Ali realised she was joking.

"My leather all-in-one cat suit and gimp mask, obviously!" Ali answered, laughing at the absurd direction this conversation was going in. There was no response, however, and she worried that maybe she had gone too far. "Hello, Blair?"

"Sorry, just banking that image to memory for future use." Another chuckle before she continued. "Right, shorts, tank and barefoot, that's all you need. When you're changed, meet me outside." Ali stood and walked to the window, looking out to see Blair sitting on her front lawn, looking relaxed in blue shorts and a white t-shirt. She was sitting on the grass, her knees slightly bent, and she was leaning back on one palm while her other hand held the phone to her ear. She was smiling, her face to the sky and eyes closed as she enjoyed the last few hours of daylight.

"Alright, I'll be out in five minutes," Ali agreed, still watching Blair as her face lit up even brighter. She looked as though she didn't have a care in the world. She was tranquil, and she looked beautiful. That thought caught Ali by surprise, but she shrugged it off.

"Oh, and Ali, there's a box on the doorstep, when you come out make sure you bring it with you. Otherwise..."

"Otherwise?" she questioned, now wondering whether it really was wise to agree to anything Blair suggested.

"You'll find out! Hurry up." Blair laughed and hung up. Ali stood still, just watching her, contemplating why it was that this woman was able to get her to agree to anything and make sure she enjoyed it.

Chapter Nineteen

A cardboard box not much bigger than a small gift box sat on the mat by itself. It had instructions printed on it.

*If you choose to complete this bucket list experience, go immediately to the kitchen, open this box, and proceed to follow the next set of instructions.*

Ali stepped outside looking for Blair, but she was nowhere to be found. She shrugged her shoulder and with a grin, turned and headed back inside the house to open the box.

Inside was a small plastic bag with 10-20 of what looked like small balloons in all different colours and a piece of paper.

*Fill each balloon with water, tie it, and when you have your weapons come outside and prepare to be soaked!*

"Are you kidding me?" Ali laughed out loud. "Water balloons? Ok, you are going down, Blair Barnes." She smirked and checked out of the window to see if she could find where Blair was hiding. No sign of her, but Ali decided that she had to be someplace where she could see the front door of the house; otherwise, she wouldn't know when Ali was coming out. Which meant that if she went out of the window at the side of the house then she could have the element of surprise. She clapped her hands gleefully and prepared her weapons.

She slid effortlessly out of the window, reached back, and grabbed her bag of water bombs, all ready to launch the moment she spotted her foe. Crouching down, she edged forward, scanning the front lawn. There weren't that many places where Blair could hide, so she took her time and studied the area. The first thing big enough to hide a grown woman was her car, but she could see completely down one side and no sign of Blair, so she slowly moved forward, keeping down in a low squat.

From here, she could see the bushes that ran down the length of the other side of the garden, plus those that were scattered through the lawn, and there she was, 30 feet away behind a large rose bush.

Ali chuckled to herself when she saw just how intently Blair was watching the door. She moved as slowly as she could and inched her way around the front of the car, her hand already reaching into her bag to grab one of the water bombs.

"Hey Blair!" she shouted, and then she launched the bomb straight at her, a direct hit to the head, the balloon bursting on impact and showering her in a cloud of cold water. She screamed and began jumping around as the icy water dripped down into places that seconds ago were hot and clammy.

Ali laughed and then ran right at her, tossing bombs that bounced on the ground and splashed up at her. When Blair turned her back to run and escape the onslaught, Ali got her with a direct hit to the butt.

Then there was a fatal mistake: she slipped on the puddle she had created and ended up on her backside. Blair stopped in her tracks and made her move. One, two, and then three balloons all hit their target as Ali squirmed and wriggled and tried to move out of the way, only for Blair to be much faster. She dropped to her knees, and before Ali knew what was happening, the blonde was straddling her waist and holding a balloon over her head. Ali looked up at her, her dry, dark hair splayed out on the grass.

"Don't you dare," Ali warned, her eyes sparkling with excitement. Her chest rose and fell with rapid breaths. Her heart was beating fast, and she wasn't quite so sure it was because of the game and not the woman looking down at her.

"Or you'll do what?" Blair teased, squeezing the balloon a little more. Ali made a grab for the balloon, but Blair was quicker and lifted out of her reach.

"No! Oh my God, Blair!" she screamed, trying to move with no success. She was well and truly pinned to the ground by firm thighs. Blair's brown eyes looking down at her sent a small shiver down her spine. Something was changing between them.

"You sneaked up on me, Ali Jenkins!" She laughed and squeezed the balloon again. "Didn't you?"

"I did, I did," Ali laughed, nodding her admission. Her only chance of escape was to give Blair what she wanted and hope she would make a fatal error, allowing her to make a move.

"And now you're going to pay." She grinned and squeezed the balloon until it burst and soaked them both. Ali shrieked with laughter. Blair relaxed, and Ali took her opportunity to try and twist out from under her, which only resulted in them lying on the grass tangled up in each other, soaked through and laughing.

Blair found herself looking down on Ali again. Her hair was all messy and wet. She reached out and pushed a strand away from her friend's face. The air between them stilled as both women continued to just stare at each other. Blair moved her palm and stroked down Ali's cheek, picking off a piece of grass that had stuck to her damp face. The urge to kiss her surged through Blair's every cell. All she had to do was lean in and then their lips would meet and it would be wonderful and arousing and...totally out of order.

"Wanna get something to eat?" she asked quickly, putting an end to those thoughts. Ali continued to stare at her before finally nodding as Blair moved off of her and stood up. She reached her hand down and helped her friend up. "Chinese?"

"Sure, whatever you want."

Chapter Twenty

It had been almost two weeks since the water fight. The days had dragged and the nights had flown by. Ali was tired; she was grumpy and miserable and bored. She had been avoiding Blair, making sure she was always 'busy' whenever she called. She only replied to email or texts with short, curt replies. But in short, she missed spending time with her.

Dealing with Blair and the way her emotions were right now had become something she just couldn't face, and everyone else was suffering because of it.

"Have you worked out what the problem is yet?" Ola asked Paula quietly. They were sitting in the staff room side by side. Ali was out of the office on a client call, and everyone was enjoying the time to take a breather and enjoy a conversation. Ali had been on their backs all week, constantly demanding from them.

"Nope, but I have noticed a lack of communication with Blair. A few weeks ago they were like peas in a pod but now, I haven't heard her talking to Blair for a good few days," Paula answered as she stood to refill her cup. She held the pot up to Ola, a silent question for her refill.

"Hmm, you think they have fallen out?" She nodded a yes, please.

"I have no idea, but it's a shame if they have. I thought maybe..." Paula left the sentence hanging. Ola understood the implication as she took back the now-full cup.

"Yes, we all did. She looked so happy recently." Taking a sip of her coffee, Ola winced. "God, we need to buy better coffee. Do you think she might be struggling with the promise?"

"Oh yeah, you ever seen them together? All holding hands and smiling at each other. I'm not sure Ali has acknowledged yet that there's an attraction there."

"Or maybe she has and that's the problem?"

~***~

Across town, Promise Hills was coming together with finishing touches and everything was on schedule for opening in just two days, as planned. Blair was in demand. Between her financial partners, new staff, and construction, she was being pulled from pillar to post. Her dream would be coming to fruition, and she should be over the moon, but she wasn't.

The water fight with Ali had been a lot of fun until she had almost kissed her. She hadn't done anything of course, but Blair was experienced enough to know when something could have happened. She had thought she had done the right thing, backing off and allowing Ali her space when all she had wanted to do was close the space between them and kiss those lips with her own. Now though, she had no idea what was going on. Ali was avoiding her, that much she understood, and usually, she would meet that kind of thing head on, but right now she had to be here at the hospice, overseeing all the people who needed to be kept on track to get this dream up and running.

So she ploughed on and watched with pride as all the signs and logos, information panels and artwork was attached to the relevant walls, windows, and ceilings. It only made her miss her friend more.

Tonight would be the official unveiling party. She should be excited about it, but she wasn't. With Ali side-stepping her, she had no idea if she would turn up tonight. All she could do was hope she would, and then maybe they could talk and fix things. She could explain how she understood her feelings would never be reciprocated, that it didn't have to come between them. Their friendship was far too important to her.

~***~

"When I ask for something to be done, I expect it to be done!" Ali hollered at Jack. Even with her door closed, the entire office could hear the reprimand. "In fact, I shouldn't even have to ask Jack, you know what the demands of this client are." She threw her pen across the desk.

"Ya know what Ali? I got no clue what is going on with you right now, but it has to stop. Get laid for fuck's sake before you alienate the entire office!" he shouted back as he stood from his chair.

"How fucking dare you! Who the hell do you think you are? Get out!" she screamed, but he was already halfway out of the door. She sat back in her chair, breathing deeply as she tried to get herself back under control.

She was well aware she wasn't the easiest person to work with at times, and there had been plenty of times over the years when she had pushed her staff to their limits, but never had any of them ever thrown something so personal at her like that. 'Get laid?' Is that what they all thought she needed?

There was a quiet rap on the door, knuckles on wood as Ola popped her head around the door pensively.

"So, ok?" she asked, a nervous smile on her face. It had been decided that someone had to go and speak to Ali, and that someone had been voted on. Ola won, or as she thought of it, lost.

Ali didn't answer right away. She sat quietly, just watching as Ola took the opportunity to enter the room properly.

"May I sit?" she asked politely, waiting until Ali nodded. "We're worried about you, Ali," she said once she was comfortable in her chair. "We know it has been a tough year for you, we understand that."

"You understand? Do you? I don't think any of you actually do understand. You all think you do, but you don't! And I hope that none of you ever do understand because it isn't a place anyone wants to find themselves." She spoke quietly, her tone even and firm.

"You're right of course, I am sorry. Maybe we shouldn't assume." She glanced down at her lap and then back at her boss. "But Ali, something is wrong and everyone can feel it. And yes, we don't understand, because we haven't done anything wrong and yet you're on our backs constantly." Ola was interrupted before she could finish her rehearsed speech.

"I'm sorry, I...there is a lot that needs to be done, and we're behind schedule on the..." She knew she was making excuses; her staff hadn't deserved her mood being taken out on them in the way she had done, and she knew why. She just didn't want to acknowledge it. She closed her eyes and took a calming breath that she blew out slowly while she considered her next sentence. "I guess I am just having a rough time at the moment with some emotions I didn't expect to be dealing with."

Ola nodded, but she didn't speak. She wasn't going to risk upsetting Ali again when it was better to just let her talk, because it looked like that was exactly what the woman needed to do.

"When Susan—" She still found the word difficult to say out loud to other people. "When she died, a part of me died with her, and now, now I find..." She couldn't find the words she needed. "I found myself feeling something that I thought had, that I thought would...and I just can't. I can't let that happen." She rambled on, and Ola let her get it out. When she stopped talking, she closed her eyes and listened.

"Ali? Nobody here is judging you. We all want you to be happy." She took a risk with her next statement. "Susan would want you to be happy, and in the past few weeks you have been happier, we've all noticed." She didn't want to push, so she waited a beat for a reply, and when none came she continued on. "What changed, Ali?"

The silence was deafening. Ali sat across the desk from her, unmoving. Ola was about to make her move to leave when she stopped dead in her tracks and sat very still.

"I was going to kiss her." The whispered words were barely audible. For a moment Ola wasn't sure she had heard her correctly, but as she looked across the desk at the blush that had settled, she knew she had heard every word.

"Why didn't you?" Ola asked gently. It didn't take a brain surgeon to work out who she was talking about, so she didn't waste time asking.

"She moved away." She smiled wistfully.

"And now you feel what?" Ola continued to probe, sitting forward in her seat.

"Guilt, embarrassment, confusion," Ali said, looking at her friend for a moment. She rubbed her hand over her face and sighed. "I feel foolish for being upset that she didn't want to, and I feel like I shouldn't be wanting anyone else anyway. It's too soon. But mainly I feel like an idiot."

"Ali, being happy doesn't have a time limit, and it certainly isn't something you should feel guilty about. Susan never wanted that. Maybe you need to read her letter again."

"I know it by heart, it doesn't change how I feel, and anyway...it doesn't matter because Blair made it clear she wasn't interested." She stood and walked to the letter, not really reading it, just looking at it. Her finger reached up and traced her late wife's name.

Ola stood too and moved towards the door. As she was leaving she turned back to Ali. "My Nigerian grandmother would say, 'A tree does not move unless there is wind.'" And then she was gone, leaving Ali to ponder the grandmother's wise words.

Chapter Twenty-One

Davina Garcia had been given the responsibility of organising the opening evening party, and she had done an amazing job from what Blair could see so far. What would in the morning become the communal room for residents was currently the setting for an informal drink for all the new staff and board members to meet the local residents and the families of the first intake of clients.

"You don't look like the new managing director of a multi-million-dollar enterprise on her opening night, darling. What's knocked the smile off your face, Blair?" Davina asked as they stood side by side at the makeshift bar.

"Hmm?" She hadn't quite understood the question until she ran it through her head once more. "Oh nothing, I am fine, tired and nervous. I'll be fine once we actually do open." She smiled quickly. Davina wasn't buying it.

"Where is that beautiful woman you were seeing? Is she not coming along to support you?" Davina was straightforward in every way. She didn't see the point in beating about the bush when you could just ask the question that you wanted answers for.

"Ali? We, I...she is just a friend. I think she must be working. She's very busy at the moment." Blair attempted to explain Ali's absence, but in truth, she was a little hurt that Ali hadn't come tonight.

"Really? The way she looks at you, I would have thought for sure you were sleeping with her." She smirked at Blair.

"No, absolutely not. Besides, I am sure that Ali has a lot of other friends to spend time with." Blair had blushed, that much Davina was sure of. She knew Blair well enough to know when she was interested in someone, and she was definitely interested in Ali Jenkins.

"So why has she just walked into the room looking like a million dollars?" Davina nudged her arm and smirked. "I'll leave you to it."

"You don't have, there's nothing to..." She stopped talking; Davina had long gone. Blair watched as she passed Ali and halted to say hello before pointing her in the right direction to find Blair and moving on.

When Ali looked towards the area Davina had pointed in, she found Blair staring directly at her. Their gaze held for much longer than it should, but neither broke the connection; Ali held the nurse's gaze as she kept moving forward until she found herself standing right in front of Blair.

The blonde looked incredible wearing a long white dress that clung perfectly to her in all the ways a dress should cling. She was wearing heels that made her taller than Ali by an inch, taller in that it put her mouth perfectly in line with Ali's own, and she knew this because her gaze had finally left Blair's eyes to drop just that little bit lower to her lips, plump kissable lips that were pouting at her. Her line of sight shifted upwards once more to find soft brown spheres that were still staring at her.

"Hi," she managed, her heart thumping wildly in her chest.

"I'm glad you came," Blair said, the urge to smile becoming overwhelming. "I didn't think you would," she admitted, the pain of that admission flashing across her face.

"I'm sorry." The apology was very much deserved, and Blair acknowledged it with a small nod and a smile. "I have been a complete bitch these past few days, and you did nothing to deserve that."

"No, I didn't, but I can forgive you, if..." She smiled wider now.

"If?" Ali asked, her own smile growing steadily as she contemplated what god-awful thing Blair was dreaming up to make her suffer.

"Yes, if you get me some champagne." A smile complemented the words.

"Is that all? I thought I was going to have to parachute off the Bank Tower!" She laughed and then realised she had just put that idea into Blair's head when she noticed her eyes light up. "Oh no, do not even think about it. I swear Blair, I am not ever throwing myself willingly off of anything, got it?" She was serious, and Blair did her best to keep up the pretence of making her do it, but the doe-eyed stare of fear eventually got the better of her, and she giggled.

"I can think of a lot of things to do to you that don't involve a parachute." She winked, and Ali relaxed a little until she realised what Blair had just said.

Ali was striking as she stood there smiling. She wore a teal sleeveless dress that stopped just short of being indecent, hugging her just like Blair found herself wanting to do.

"Maybe I will let you," Ali countered before turning and walking toward the barman to get them both a glass of champagne, leaving Blair to think about it.

~***~

The evening had been a success for Blair. Davina had encouraged her to make a speech and officially open the building, which was not something she was particularly comfortable with, but she did it anyway. She thanked her backers for their belief in the project and their unyielding support to get the venture up and running, no matter the cost or the hoops they had had to jump through in order to get things signed off. She also thanked her new staff members for their passion and commitment to help her achieve everything that Promise Hills was set up to do. She welcomed the support from the local community and offered her most sincere promise to do all she could for the clients that chose to enjoy Promise Hills, and lastly, she thanked Ali for not only providing the expertise and imagination in designing the signage of the building, but in doing so for free; it had allowed for an extra budget option for day trips and bucket list events. But mostly, she thanked her for the support and encouragement she had given her during this hectic time.

~***~

"You didn't have to say all that." Ali blushed as Blair joined her once more.

"Yes, I did." She smiled and reached for her hand, relieved when Ali allowed her to take it. "What you did for us was wonderful enough, but what you've done for me, being there when I needed someone and entertaining me too!" She couldn't take her eyes from Ali's. The smiles on their faces only made the moment more enjoyable.

"I think the bucket list idea is wonderful."

"I was inspired by Susan," she said, and Ali teared up a little. "Can we get out of here?"

"You want to leave your own party?" Ali said. There were still a lot of people in the room, and she had expected to be here for a while with Blair, if she wanted her to be. Blair let go of her hand to take two more glasses of champagne as the waitress walked by, passing one to Ali.

"Yeah, well maybe just a walk in the grounds," Blair suggested, realising she couldn't just leave. She felt fingers link with her own, looked down to see that Ali had taken her hand, and felt the tug as Ali began leading her out of the room.

~***~

It was dark outside, or it would have been if it weren't for the motion-sensor security lights that flashed on as they walked the pathways away from the building. They were still holding hands, arms brushing against one another as they strolled amiably along. It was a comfortable silence as they took a turn to the left.

The beautifully manicured lawns and flowerbeds in the moonlight were magical, the pathways paved in order for wheelchairs to be pushed comfortably without jarring the person sitting in them, and benches dotted around for anyone who just wanted to sit and contemplate or enjoy the view.

"Ya know you did a really great job here, Blair?" Ali said as they came to a stop by the fountain. The sound of the water trickling gently was relaxing, just like it was supposed to be.

"Thank you, it means a lot to me that you think so." Blair turned, her body still close enough to Ali that she could feel the heat emanating from her, her fingers linked tightly around Ali's. "You mean a lot to me, Ali."

"I know, I—" Ali could feel the intensity building, the unwavering need she had to feel close to this woman. Blair felt it too and knew she needed to do something after messing it all up following the water balloons catastrophe. She could see Ali was going to kiss her, and she had panicked and tried to swerve away from the situation with the offer of dinner, words that had hurt Ali, she knew that much now.

"Do you think maybe we should talk about it?" Blair asked.

"I don't know how to," Ali replied.

"I think maybe..." Blair looked at her for a moment, trying to decide something. She nodded to herself, seemingly coming to a conclusion with a small smile. "Ali, I think that..." Words were not going to work, not right now; she was past words. So, she did the only thing she knew how: she leant forward and slowly, so slowly she thought her heart had stopped beating, allowed her lips to make contact with Ali's mouth. Her eyes closed as she felt her own lips close gently around the soft pouting lip of her friend.

She waited, fearing that she had made a mistake when Ali didn't immediately kiss her back, but then finally, Ali caught up. Her hand rose to take Blair's face in her palm as the kiss became more, as her lips began to move against the softness. Blair felt the light swipe of Ali's tongue, and with no further thought, she permitted the intrusion with a soft groan of hunger, hunger for the woman finally in her arms.

Chapter Twenty-Two

*"Kissing you is like kissing a marshmallow," Susan laughed, licking her lips before pulling her wife back into her to continue the kiss. "God, I could do this for hours." She breathed a deep satisfied sigh.*

*"Well, we don't have to be anywhere, so—" Ali grinned and claimed her mouth once more. When the kiss finally broke, she opened her eyes and Blair stood smiling at her, lipstick smeared across her cheek.*

It was dark, the room cold and silent as she tossed the covers from her and sat up on the edge of the bed. A light sweat covered her face, and she wiped at her eyes as she tried to push the dream from her mind. She dragged her hand through her long hair before standing and walking naked to the bathroom. A slight shiver coursed its way down her spine as she pulled the light switch and stood in front of the mirror.

It was the same spot she had stood in hours earlier when she had arrived home from the party. She had left right after the kiss, much to the dismay of Blair, who had remained motionless, confused and probably hurt, Ali had assumed. Which was exactly how Ali felt.

Blair had kissed her, and Ali had liked it and kissed her back. She had wanted it, needed it, and didn't refuse it, but then all at once the guilt hit her and she couldn't breathe. She needed to get out of there and process it all.

She went back to her room and flopped down onto the bed. Lying there in the dark, she tried to clear her mind, but all she could think about was Blair and that kiss. Because she felt it. She felt it in every nerve ending and cell. It was like electricity flowing through her veins, and she wanted to do it again.

"I like her," she whispered into the darkness.

The clock on her phone read just gone three a.m., and she noticed the text message that had come through.

**>Blair: Hey, I just wanted to make sure you got home ok. I think maybe it would be good to talk, tomorrow?**

~***~

But tomorrow didn't work out. The opening of Promise Hills kept Blair chained to her desk. She hadn't seen Ali since the night of the party, and it was driving her a little bit crazy. She wanted to talk, to discuss the kiss and where it left them, but with new clients to settle and employee issues to deal with as everything began to fall into place, she hadn't been able to get away. Her days had been long and tiring so far with early starts and late finishes, meaning she slept the few hours in between.

To her credit, Ali hadn't run. She had continued to be supportive and encourage Blair; however, she hadn't mentioned the kiss, and that worried Blair a little.

She had just completed her last rounds of the rooms and ensured everything was as it should be, clocking up a lot of steps on her Fitbit as she wandered the corridors all day. As she opened the door to her office, intent on sitting down and getting her shoes off for a few minutes, she couldn't help but smile.

Ali sat in her chair waiting for her, her feet up on the desk, crossed at the ankles as though she owned it. She was wearing dark blue skinny jeans and a crisp white tee shirt complementing it.

"Well, I figured if you weren't going to find any time to see me, then I should probably find time to see you." She pulled her feet down from the desk and, leaning to her left, she lifted a picnic basket that she placed on the desk. "I assume you haven't eaten yet?"

Blair shook her head and moved closer to the desk. Ali glanced at her and smiled. "I guess you want your chair back?" she laughed as she stood, walking toward where Blair stood motionless. "Hi."

"Hello," Blair acknowledged, still a little dumbfounded.

"This is where you kiss me," Ali whispered, enjoying the way she had Blair a little perplexed. The blonde leant forward and placed a chaste but warm kiss against her lips, enjoying the feel of Ali kissing her back. "I'm sorry, should I have called first. I just thought it would be nice to—" Ali was cut off mid-sentence by soft warm lips that pressed against hers with an energy she hadn't felt in a long time. Blair pushed her gently backwards until she felt the hard edge of the desk behind her. It was intense, physical, as hands began to move and explore. When the need for air became too much and they broke apart gasping, Blair pressed her forehead to Ali's.

"Sorry, I—" she began, but Ali placed a finger to her lips.

"Don't, don't apologise, please. This is hard enough for me without you being sorry about it. I need you to not be sorry that you kissed me. Can you do that for me?" Ali said, her gaze intense. Blue crystal eyes bore into Blair as she nodded. "Ok?"

"Ok." And it was ok. "So, what have we got for dinner?" Blair asked, sitting down at the desk in the visitor's chair, leaving her own chair free for Ali, who dragged it around the blockage so she could sit with Blair.

"Well, I had some time on my hands, so I cooked up a chicken casserole and some apple pie."

"Really? You cooked? For me?" Blair asked, her eyes lighting up a little.

"Oh yes, I am quite adept in the kitchen now, don't you know." She smiled as she pulled out the Tupperware dish full of delicious chicken. The smell that wafted up was amazing, and Blair suddenly realised just how famished she was. "So, what time do you plan to finish working tonight?" Ali asked as she pulled dishes and cutlery from the basket, placing them all on the desk. Blair sighed and rubbed her tired face.

"I don't know, technically I should be done now, but..." She watched as Ali shared the casserole between two bowls and handed one to her. "I just need to make sure everything is ok."

"Do you trust your staff?" Ali asked as she spooned a mouthful.

"Yes, I think so, yes." Blair did the same and savoured the flavour. "This is delicious." The compliment made Ali beam at her. She made a mental note to make that happen more often.

"I think you should come home with me," Ali said, her gaze never leaving Blair. "You need to get away from here and let your staff do their job before you exhaust yourself and drive them crazy."

"But—"

"No, no buts Blair. It's my turn to kidnap you, so eat up and then we are going back to my place, or yours if you prefer, and we're going to relax with a movie and maybe practice this snuggling thing that I miss so much." And there was no arguing with that kind of offer.

~***~

Comfortable. That was the word Ali would use to describe the feelings she had while being wrapped in Blair's arms. They had decided to go to Blair's place. She, after all, had to go to work in the morning, and Ali didn't. The couch was comfortable as she felt herself sink into soft cushions. She was beginning to enjoy being the little spoon with Blair. She had never even contemplated it before now and yet, it was perfect.

Blair's arm wrapped tightly around her, and she held her hand within her grasp. She could feel her breath hot and gentle against her neck, and it too was relaxing. They had moved straight to the couch as soon as they had entered the apartment, talking very little as they both relaxed and just enjoyed each other's company.

The briefest kiss placed on her shoulder by Blair sent a shiver down her spine as she relaxed back against her. When she saw no hint of displeasure, Blair did it again, this time with a little more pressure, a little longer. She moved slowly, her movements gentle and thoughtful as her lips caressed the skin available to them, along her shoulder and upward toward an earlobe. Ali turned and looked at her. Studying her, she allowed her hand to reach up and pull Blair toward her, initiating a more tender and passionate kiss. Their lips connected, pushing and tugging at each other until both parted and slick hot tongues clamoured to explore.

Blair's fingers brushed slowly against her cheek. Soft moans echoed through the room as both women lost themselves in the kiss. Ali felt the ghostlike touch come across her chest, her breast, down her stomach until soft fingertips made contact with hot skin and pushed up under her shirt, the touch electric.

Her muscles tightened and quivered at the feeling of somebody else's palm caressing her, moving higher to cup her breast, the nipple instantly hardening.

*"What are you doing?" Ali asked as Susan lay against her, her fingers dancing up and down her abs and chest.*

*"Nothing," she said quietly as she continued the movements, her lover's skin dimpling with each gentle caress. "I just like the way your body reacts to me."*

Gasping for air, Ali broke the kiss, her palm pressing gently against Blair's chest.

"Wait, sorry I—" She took deep breaths and looked into the concerned eyes of her...girlfriend? "I'm sorry, I..." She tried to sit up, and Blair adjusted herself so she could do so, instantly aware that something had changed.

"Hey, it's ok," Blair whispered. "You don't have to apologise, we can go slowly, yeah?" Ali nodded with a grateful smile.

"I just, I haven't..." She struggled to explain. "I haven't, ya know, with anyone, not since—"

"Since Susan? I know, I understand. It's fine, Ali." Blair kissed her forehead, stroked her face and pushed her hair back behind her ear. She was gentle and loving with her movements. "We don't have to—"

"But I want to, I really want to, I just..." She pulled Blair back into her, her fingers tangling in Blair's hair as she kissed her mouth once more. "I just, it's new." She kissed her harder, desperately pulling her hand back against her, under her shirt and then pushing downwards, forcing Blair's hand under the band of her jeans. The blonde tried to pull her hand free only to have Ali hold her in place.

"Please, I want to, I need..." She pressed her forehead against Blair and stared intently. "Touch me."

"Ali, this isn't—" Blair held her own hand still. "I want you. I want so much to be with you in this way, but not like this." She finally freed her hand and cupped her potential lover's face. "Not like this."

Chapter Twenty-Three

Ali read through her bucket list. There were still quite a few things to do, and she had encouraged Blair to hand over hers so that they could coordinate and maybe do one or two this weekend. While Blair finished her shift that Friday morning, Ali lay the two pieces of paper side by side on the table next to her morning coffee.

She was still at Blair's, having spent the night, although they had only slept side by side. She felt as though she were reaching a point of no return and it scared her to her bones. Everything was so confusing; her emotions were scattered. Blair had been right to stop them, to stop her from taking things further. It was too soon. She understood that this wasn't just about sex. There were Blair's feelings that had to be considered too. The last thing she wanted to do was end up hurting Blair.

She breathed in deeply and then released it quickly. There was nothing she could do right now but spend time with Blair and see where life took them. Sipping her coffee, she pulled her list forward and read it.

Get a tattoo
~~Send a message in a bottle~~
~~Finish a crossword~~
Turn my phone off for 24 hours

Leave a $100 tip

Go on a hike

~~Read a book cover to cover in one sitting.~~

Go away for the weekend

Give my heart to someone

She read through it twice more before switching her attention to Blair's list. She smiled as she read the first on the list; such a romantic. The thought of kissing Blair in the rain suddenly became something she couldn't stop thinking about, but the rain didn't happen very often in California, so she concentrated on some of the other things on their lists that they could do.

Kiss someone in the rain

~~Visit a nudist beach~~

Go on a hike

Take a weekend off

~~Have a water balloon fight~~

Fly a plane

Go see strippers

~~Break the law~~

So far, they seemed to have done quite a lot, slightly more on Blair's list, but then she considered Blair had been more than eager to participate in the bucket list adventure and Ali had to admit, it had been fun so far. It was only fair that she put as much effort into it as Blair had been.

Looking back and forth, she realised there were two things they both seemed to agree on, and it wasn't beyond the realms of possibility to arrange, although she had no intention of ever doing the flying a plane idea.

Grabbing her phone, she quickly texted Blair. She felt herself smiling as she typed and realised she was at least enjoying this relationship with Blair, regardless of where it eventually led.

**>Ali: I know it's short notice but, with it being Friday today, are you able to make yourself free for the weekend?**

Ali had a plan developing in her mind, and if Blair gave the go-ahead, she figured they would both be knocking quite a few things off the lists. But first, she needed to get dressed, which she might as well do once she got home because she would need to pack and use her computer if she was to get this off the ground.

~***~

Blair heard her phone beep to alert her to a message as she was dealing with a young man who was coming to the end of his life way too early for anyone to be comfortable with it. However, it was Blair and her team's job to make sure it happened with dignity, and they had maintained that to the very best of their ability. Jonathon was supported by his parents and siblings. They were a wonderful family from what Blair could tell, and they appreciated the hands-on approach Blair brought to their son's care.

So, it was gone lunchtime when she was able to get a chance to look at her messages. She skipped them all once she noticed the one from Ali. Smiling, she flicked the screen open and replied.

**>Blair: Actually, I think that might be a great idea. It has been a tough morning.**

She sent the message and then set about organising her staff to be available while she took off. The joys of being the boss, she told herself, and it didn't hurt that she would be spending her time with Ali. The thought of spending the weekend with the gorgeous brunette had sent her excitement levels into overdrive.

~***~

Ali had been busy. She logged on to the computer and began scouring her options as soon as she was showered and dressed again. Booking a hotel room was simple enough; she had the perfect place to visit. She just hoped that Blair would be as excited about it as she was.

>Ali: You need to pack enough clothes for two nights, outfits for walking and for dining, and be here to pick me up in an hour?

Blair giggled as she read the message, an hour? She had literally just walked through the door. She checked her watch, she had basically 30 minutes to get her stuff together.

**>Blair: Challenge accepted.**

~***~

When Blair arrived, Ali felt that same gentle tug in her tummy that she used to feel with Susan, that instant arousal. It wasn't quite the wrench she was used to feeling, but it was there, and it was growing. Without any hesitation, Blair pulled her into her arms, kissing her gently on the lips and then the forehead.

"So, what are you planning to do with me?" she inquired with a raised brow.

"Oh, well I figured a little trip. We both have a weekend away on our list, and we both want to hike, so..." Suddenly she became a little nervous. Maybe she had gone too far and Blair wouldn't want to spend a weekend away with her.

"What is it?" Blair asked, moving to look her straight in the eye. God, she could look into those eyes forever and just let herself get lost in them, but she focused, forced herself to keep her attention on the words Ali was speaking from those luscious lips. Oh dear God, she berated herself internally. Focus!

"I booked us a room," Ali said quietly. A room, not us rooms, but a room.

"Ok, I can cope with you for a couple of nights," Blair smirked.

"Yeah? I mean I know we don't – we're taking things slowly, but it just seemed silly to pay for two rooms when, well I liked sleeping with you last night," she admitted, much to Blair's amusement as she stepped closer, her hands reaching up to finger the delicate collar of her shirt.

"Yeah?" Blair said, her arms sliding around Ali's waist, easily pulling her closer.

"Yeah." She smiled shyly and allowed Blair to bring their lips together in a tender kiss. There it was again, that gentle tug deep down in her tummy.

Chapter Twenty-Four

Leaving home by three p.m., they were both checked into their room by eight. It had been a long drive, and they had stopped only once for a coffee and bathroom break.

The conversation had flowed easily between them. They shared the driving. When Ali drove, Blair's palm rested gently on Ali's thigh. When Blair drove, Ali would turn in her seat and lean into Blair, laughing at her lame jokes. She touched her face, kissed her cheek. With every mile they drove, they both became more comfortable.

The room Ali had booked for the night was lovely. There was a bed of course, and a bathroom with a full bath and walk-in shower. It was a small room, but that didn't matter because they didn't plan to be here very much.

Dinner was booked for nine p.m., and that meant they had no time to explore the area beforehand, not if they wanted to get changed and look their best, which was what Ali had in mind when she booked the restaurant. She wanted a chance to dress up again. This would be a first date, something to remember, and she wanted to make it special.

Blair had showered first, and while Ali took her turn, Blair changed into her new dress, a rather expensive and impulsive treat she had happened upon a few weeks ago. It suited her perfectly; the colour worked well with her skin tone, and the style accentuated every inch of her that was worthy of flaunting. It dipped low on her cleavage and high on her thighs. It clung perfectly to her hips, and the short sleeves emphasised her toned arms. She let her blonde hair hang loosely around her face, but kept nervously tucking one side behind her ear.

Ali had taken her clothes into the bathroom with her, intending to dress once showered and leave Blair in peace. However, she had forgotten one vital element in her plan: underwear. So, she wrapped the towel around herself and quickly popped back into the bedroom.

Hearing the sound of the bathroom door opening behind her, Blair twisted around to find Ali stopped in her tracks. They both stared at one another as Blair realised Ali was half-naked and Ali realised just how stunning Blair was.

"Wow, you look—" Ali was almost speechless, but she managed to get it together in time to add, "beautiful."

"Thank you." Blair blushed. Biting her lip, she added, "You look...underdressed." Then she smiled and turned fully, watching as Ali remembered what she was wearing.

"Ah yes, I forgot—" She held her underwear up to show rather than say. "I'll just be—" She pointed to the bathroom and retreated, unable to take her eyes off of the woman in front of her.

~***~

Behind the safety of the bathroom door she leant against, Ali felt her pulse racing as she tried to get a hold of herself. Closing her eyes, she breathed deeply.

"Have you never seen a gorgeous woman before?" Susan asked, laughing at the way Ali had fawned over the actress that had been sitting next to them at the theatre.

"Of course I have, I see you every single day." She smirked back, aware that she had just been caught by her wife behaving like a love-struck teenager. "But that was Shelly Hamlin, in the flesh I might add."

"Ah yes, and here I was thinking she was unimportant." Susan continued to find the entire episode humorous. "Shall I wait while you ask her on a date?"

"Oh ha ha." Ali frowned, and Susan could tell if she pushed it much further then there would be a full-on sulk.

"She is very beautiful, I really do understand your attraction. I don't mind, honestly." She kissed Ali and walked past to open the car door. "Don't be long. You can only admire her for a moment and then she will be gone."

There was no denying it anymore. She was completely attracted to Blair in every way. She was aroused by her, stimulated by her. Blair could entertain her, make her laugh, soothe her. Everything anyone would want from another person, she knew she could have with Blair. She had promised Susan that she would try, and that's what she was going to do.

~***~

The restaurant was close by, and they had walked the short distance hand in hand. It felt the most natural thing, to put her hand within Blair's. Ali wondered briefly if she really could put her heart in Blair's hands too. Her thoughts were interrupted when she felt Blair squeeze gently. She glanced across at her.

The blonde was smiling at her. "Everything okay?"

Ali nodded. "I think so." She returned the smile.

"You look a little pensive," Blair suggested, still smiling.

They stopped walking and Ali looked away, searching for the right words. When she turned back, the words just flowed. "I guess that I am in a state of flux. It's like I have two lives, the one I live with Susan...and then there is the one I think I could have..." Her eyes rose up to look at Blair, her expressive brown eyes now looking at her with hope shining from them. "With you."

"I get that. I'm just glad that you at least see me as someone that you potentially could move forward with."

"I do. I like you very much, Blair."

"Good, because I like you a lot too, Ali."

"I know, and that's what worries me."

Blair frowned at her, her eyes suddenly saddened.

"I...the last thing I want to do is hurt you. This...whatever this is between us...I can't promise you that—"

"Ali? Let's just enjoy each day as it comes, okay?" Blair interrupted her before she said what she already knew was a possibility.

Ali nodded. "Yes, okay." Blair smiled.

~***~

The restaurant was quite busy. It appeared as though everyone in town was eating out tonight. They sat opposite one another at a square table, sipping water while they waited for their dinner.

Ali looked across the table at Blair. She had been rather quiet these past few minutes. She reached a hand across, touching Blair to get her attention.

"I'm sorry, have I ruined things?"

"What? No." Blair shook her head. "No, absolutely not, Ali. I'm enjoying our time together."

"Me too, I just...I know that this must be frustrating for you."

"It's not," Blair said, taking her hand. "I know the risk...I know that when all is said and done, you might never be in a place to let me love you, but while I have the chance to find out, then I want to."

"I'm trying." Ali smiled.

"I know. I guess though I have something else on my mind that I probably should talk with someone about," Blair admitted.

"So talk to me." Ali squeezed her hand. "You can always talk to me, unless of course you're just dating me for the not having sex and amusing days out?" They both laughed. The waitress arrived with their order, and they spent the rest of the evening enjoying the company and talking.

Blair explained to Ali about Jonathon and how much of a toll it would take on the staff when they lost someone. Even though it was what they expected and knew would happen, Jonathon would be the first for Promise Hills.

It felt good being able to share this with Ali, knowing she understood the stress and upset losing a patient would cause Blair and her staff, and knowing she would have that shoulder to lean on when the time came.

But she didn't want to dwell on it; it was a lovely evening so far, and when they had finished the last mouthful of dessert and swallowed the last remnants of the wine they had ordered, Blair paid the bill and they left, once more hand in hand as they took in the sights Las Vegas had to offer.

"I am having a really nice time," Blair offered as they passed by the numerous sights and sounds of various hotels and shows along the strip.

"Me too," Ali responded, squeezing the hand she held. It was a nice night, warm still. They passed tourists and locals as they filed past on the hunt for the next fun place to play and giggled at some of the more outrageous personalities.

"Do I get to know what else you have planned? You said something about knocking several items off the bucket lists."

"I did, didn't I?" Ali chuckled. "Ok well, we have now knocked off the getting away for the weekend, and I switched my phone off, which was on my list. 24 hours with no cell," she explained. "And tomorrow I thought we could go and see the Grand Canyon and take a short hike, and that would knock that off the list also."

"Great, anything else?" Blair asked, smiling now as she watched the brunette alongside her become animated.

"You'll see," she teased, pulling Blair's hand in the direction she wanted to go.

~***~

They walked for what felt like minutes but was actually a mile as they continued to converse and laugh with each other, learning facts about one another that would pull them closer together in the long run. The bright lights of Vegas lit up their faces as each of them understood just how much they really did enjoy each other's company.

"Are you drunk at all?" asked Ali as she stopped them on the sidewalk. "Only, they won't let us do what I have planned if either of us is too inebriated."

"Ok, now you have my attention, and no I am not drunk. I was a little tipsy when we left the restaurant, but I feel fine now."

"Good, then we're going in here," she said, pointing over her shoulder. Blair turned slowly, eyes widening as she took in the words 'Tattoo Studio'.

"Oh no," she groaned, "No, no, no."

"Come on, this was your idea, Blair." Ali laughed at the look of pure horror on her friend's face.

"You really want to do this?" she gulped, trying to put on a brave face.

"Yes, but if you don't, then—"

"No, I said I would." Blair sucked in a breath and stopped herself from contemplating it any further. "And that's what we will do, do you know what you want?" Blair accepted her fate, already knowing she would probably do whatever this beautiful, bright, and fun woman asked her to.

"I do, I'm going to have an infinity symbol entwined with a rose and a little bee," she revealed, her eyes smiling.

*"You got me roses? I love roses,"* Susan gushed when Ali arrived on their first official date.

*"Well, I saw these and I thought how beautiful they were and they reminded me of you and that if tonight is as successful as I hope it will be, then our love will be infinite."*

*"I am already in love with you, so I think tonight is a given,"* she replied, pulling Ali into the house while her hand slid around the back of her neck and brought Ali's lips crashing against her own.

"And what am I going to have?" Blair asked, smitten and ready to mark her flesh with Ali.

"Well, that's for you to decide, but I can help you pick if want?"

"I do want, I want you—" she began. "Actually, that's all, I want you." She tried to smile, but nerves got the better of her as she realised the seriousness of what she had just said out loud.

Ali only studied her, her eyes scanning Blair's face, searching for something that Blair could only hope she found, thoughts drifting through her mind on a conveyor belt of emotions. Blair

237

waited, just like the night in the gardens of Promise Hills when she had kissed Ali, and she watched as this time Ali stepped forward and tentatively kissed her. The kiss was delicate, like a whisper on the breeze. She felt the touch of fingertips as Ali caressed her cheek.

"I want that too," she whispered. "I'm just not there yet."

Blair nodded and smiled. She hadn't said no.

Chapter Twenty-Five

Waking the following morning wrapped once again in Blair's embrace, Ali couldn't help but smile as she remembered back to the previous night.

*"I don't want it too big, ok?" Blair gave her instructions to the tattooist who nodded and began to draw out the design Blair had picked: two hearts entwined around the caduceus.*

*"Blair, do you need me to hold your hand or will you be a big girl?" Ali had laughed, earning a glare from the blonde.*

*"I think I can cope, thank you, Ali," she had said, a cocky grin on her face; after all, she had watched Ali get hers, and it hadn't seemed to bother the brunette too much. The tattooist asked her if she was happy with the design and, with the go-ahead, began to ink the outline. "Holy fucking crap," Blair swore loudly, reaching for Ali, who took her hand instantly, stifling a giggle. "You didn't tell me it was this painful."*

*"What can I say? No pain, no gain." Ali finally laughed until she felt Blair squeeze her hand so tightly she thought her fingers might break.*

She felt the warm arm tighten around her, the ink mark inches from her lips. She kissed the area next to it and felt the body stir behind her.

"I am never listening to you again," Blair mumbled against Ali's shoulder, only the cotton covering of her nightwear between them.

"I'm sorry."

"No, you're not." Blair smiled against her now, before pressing her lips against her neck.

"No, I am not. I like it, it looks—" She thought for the right word. "Sexy."

"Sexy huh? Okay, I can live with that."

~***~

Ali and Blair left Vegas as soon as they were dressed. The air conditioning in the car was permanently on as they drove the I-40 east towards the Grand Canyon. It was a desolate route, for the most part, just sand and heat. The temperature gauge in the car read 100.4.

"It's unbearable," Ali said. Blair was driving, the road ahead clear, so she kept the car travelling at a smooth 70 mph. Even with the air conditioner on, it was still hot.

"It is surprising how much hotter it is now that we're out of the city." She chanced a glance across at Ali. She seemed pretty relaxed. She was wearing a simple yellow strappy top and white cotton shorts, her hair was tied back, and she wore a pair of sunglasses that Blair had made fun of. Sophia Loren would have been proud to wear them. They were huge, but she looked good.

"Weird huh? Must be all that air conditioning in every building filtering out into the air." She smiled. Blair was looking at her and smiling too. "What are you smiling at?"

"Nothing, just looking at you," Blair said, her focus returning back to the road ahead. Still no traffic, just them and the sand and of course, the heat. "You're beautiful."

Ali was quiet and Blair worried that she had pushed it too far. She was trying so very hard to keep things slow, allowing Ali to get there in her own time, and yet, every thought she had involved Ali now. All she wanted was to show Ali just how much she cared and wanted her.

"I'm sorry, I didn't mean to—" She began to apologise, but was stopped when Ali spoke at the same time.

"It's fine, I just find it difficult—" They both laughed, and Blair nodded for her to continue. "I've never really been very good at accepting compliments. Susan used to give them all the time and I would brush them off."

"Okay, noted, but I can't promise that I won't give them anyway." Blair grinned.

They were quiet again for several miles. Blair could tell that Ali was debating something. She could almost hear the whirring of clogs as the mechanics of her brain clicked into action. She wanted to ask, wanted to delve into that intelligent mind and hear all it had to say, but she waited. The radio was playing a country song she recognised, so she hummed along.

"We were going to have kids, ya know?" Ali said, a statement completely out of the blue.

"Yeah, I think Susan mentioned that."

"We had all these dreams, everything planned out." She looked out of the window. There were small clumps of greenery now, and billboards advertising lawyers and accident repair. "Everyone thinks you just lose the person, that once you've grieved you'll be over it, able to move forward, but nobody ever thinks about the rest of it. The hopes, the dreams you have, all the plans you made together that are suddenly gone too." This time her eyes were closed, a lone tear sliding down her cheek.

Blair pulled the car over to the side of the road and put it into park. She twisted in her seat to face Ali.

"Ali?" She spoke gently and reached out to touch her arm. "Ali, I don't know what I can say to make you feel better. I know that I am not Susan and that all of those dreams you shared together have come to a halt for you, and I'm sorry, I am so sorry that you have to deal with any of this." She could feel her own tears welling in her eyes as she kept Ali in her sights.

Without moving, Ali spoke. "It's just strange. It's been..." She inhaled and exhaled. "We would have...I would be a mother now." She smiled sadly and turned to Blair.

"Is that something that you still want?" They were holding hands; it felt warm and safe. A lorry drove by them at speed and the vehicle rocked gently.

"I don't know," Ali answered. "We were going to adopt. We were just waiting..." She sobbed and fell into Blair's arms. "Waiting for the right time. I am always waiting for the right time, and...there was no time. There was no time, Blair."

"Oh Ali." She couldn't argue with Ali's thoughts. There was nothing she could say to make things better; easier. All she could do was just hold her, let her cry it out and be there afterwards. She kissed the side of Ali's head and rocked her gently until finally, she quieted.

Chapter Twenty-Six

The views of the Grand Canyon were beyond exquisite, far-reaching and expansive. The clear blue of a cloudless sky gave way to the vast redness of rock as it wound its way, gauging through the earth as though a giant hand had dragged a finger through soft mud. People stood in awe, admiring the sheer magnitude of the place. They sat and contemplated what they were seeing, while others grinned like idiots as they sat on the edge of overhanging rocks.

It was hot still in the early afternoon as they walked the Bright Angel Trail, but thankfully the winding pathways that led them around the rim were often in a fair amount of shade that gave some respite.

Blair had made sure to stop as often as possible while she snapped away with her phone, capturing some of the most spectacular views she and Ali had ever seen.

"Can you believe how beautiful it is here?" Ali gasped, in awe as she looked around them. They had stopped near a cliff edge that had a clear view as far as the eye could see. She was feeling much better since her impromptu crying episode three hours earlier. It felt good to acknowledge everything that had been floating around in the back of her mind, so many things she had pushed away and refused to think about.

The dusty terrain gave way to sloping precipices and rising rocky cliffs. More daring visitors climbed down in order to stand on overhanging rocks, armed with selfie sticks and no plan on how to climb back up again.

"Yes, you would be amazed at how often I get to enjoy beauty around me." Blair grinned, snapping a quick picture of Ali. She watched as Ali turned slowly, aware suddenly of Blair's words. Her cheeks, pink already from the sun beating down on them, reddened a little more.

"Such a charmer." She smiled and reached for Blair's hand. Fingers linked as they continued onwards, together.

Bright Angel Trail was an old trading route for trappers and early settlers, so the pathways were well-trodden, easily walked by two hand-holding women with all the time in the world to enjoy it, and each other. Its landscape changed from serene to dramatic from one turn of the road to the next.

After three miles of walking, they came across another resting spot and took a well-earned break. Ali reached into the bag she was carrying and pulled out a bottle of water, taking a long drink before passing it over to Blair.

"Thanks." She grasped the cold bottle and swallowed down a huge swig, the coolness of the liquid refreshing every cell in her body. "Man, that's good."

They sat quietly on a rock side by side, their pinkies linking together, connecting them without either even realising.

*"If you want to kiss me, you can, ya know,"* Susan whispered as she leaned against Ali's shoulder while they sat on the wall at the end of her garden. Their first date had been a success in her opinion.

*"Who says I want to?"* Ali teased, her eyes twinkling with mischief.

*"It's all you can think about."*

The brunette found herself staring at Blair. A piece of loose hair had gotten her attention and drawn her into enjoying the profile of the woman currently occupying her thoughts. She had her eyes closed, her face into the sunlight as she licked her lower lip from the dryness of the air around them.

"Blair?"

"Yeah?" she answered without moving, but when no reply came she opened her eyes and turned to look at Ali. She found herself caught, unable to look away from the brunette as those blue eyes focused solely on her. She watched as slowly, Ali moved forward, inching ever closer before the softness of her lips pressed against Blair's. Blair found herself surprised when Ali smiled into the kiss and swiped her tongue across the path Blair's own tongue had recently mapped, deepening the embrace.

When the kiss ended, Ali blushed and looked away quickly until Blair caught her chin and gently brought her back to face her.

"You don't have to feel guilty for kissing me, Ali," she said gently as Ali forced herself to look at the big brown eyes that swept across her face reverently.

"That's just it, Blair." Her fingers reached out and finally placed the errant piece of hair back behind Blair's ear. "I'm not sure that I do feel guilty, but, I feel guilty about that." She laughed ironically. "That doesn't even make any sense, does it?"

"Yes, it does. Of course it does. You want to kiss me, I want to kiss you too, so I understand."

"But—"

"Uh-uh, no buts Ali. It's ok. We agreed to go slow and at your pace, I am okay with that, and however long it takes for you to feel a hundred percent okay with us, that's how long I'll wait."

~***~

Hiking back along the trail as the sun began to descend in the sky was even more spectacular than anything either had ever seen before. The sky was so many hues of oranges and reds that it appeared to be on fire. Rays of sunlight draped down the cliff edges in a last drastic attempt to linger.

They found a flat rock and sat down to watch, Ali cocooned once more between Blair's thighs and arms. She felt safe there perched on the edge of a cliff embraced with warmth. Relaxing, she felt herself melt against Blair's strong hold on her, felt the softness of lips kiss the side of her head as she sighed softly and just went with the feeling.

It was an awesome experience, and it would stay with them both for years to come. Ali realised she was building memories,

memories that wouldn't include Susan, memories that involved Blair Barnes instead. And just for today, she was okay with that.

~***~

The car ride to their next hotel was filled with music and singing. Old hits of the 90s that Blair barely knew mixed in with hits of the day and some old favourites from Ali's iPod.

"I can't believe you have never heard of Bon Jovi," Ali declared, realising that maybe a six-year age gap had more surprises than she had bargained for.

"I didn't say I hadn't heard of them!!" Blair burst out laughing. "I just don't know the words or the songs."

"Well that just makes me feel old." The laughter that poured from Blair now was contagious, and Ali found herself chuckling too.

"You're not old. Well, not ancient anyway," Blair teased, receiving a gentle slap on her thigh.

"You are so in trouble."

"I hope so," Blair flirted, unable to stop herself from enjoying this moment of banter. Before Ali could reply, the next song burst out of the speakers and she instantly began singing along. Blair found herself mesmerised. She enjoyed witnessing this fun side of Ali. It was obvious to everyone that something was lifting for Ali. Happiness was invading rather than evading her.

Chapter Twenty-Seven

It was Saturday night in a sleepy little town in the middle of nowhere a few miles away from the Canyon. Their hotel room was nothing like the plush modern style of Vegas that Ali had loved, but it was just as wonderful: homely and clean, rustic. That was how Ali would describe it as they both fell through the door laughing at something funny they had both noticed when they had pulled up outside and parked the car. Not daring to look at one another while checking in, they had been unable to contain it once the key had opened the door.

"Oh God, I didn't think she would ever stop talking," Blair gasped, catching her breath and holding her sides from all the giggling.

"If you had dared to look at me, I don't think I could have controlled myself," Ali answered, throwing her case down on the bed and collapsing next to it.

"I've never seen anything like it." She placed her own case down next to the bed and sat beside Ali, still smiling.

"It certainly is a unique hairstyle," Ali said, her lips curling again, ready to laugh once more as she turned slightly to face Blair. Sliding her hands up into her own hair, she lifted it and scrunched it into a replica of the woman's style. "What do you think?" She laughed hard and fell backwards onto the bed.

"It cannot be real, I mean it would need an entire can of spray to keep it up that high!" Blair could hold it in no longer and fell back in fits of giggles too. "Maybe there is something living in it?"

When the giggling finally subsided, Blair realised that Ali had moved closer and was now snuggled against her right-hand side. She had placed her arm across Blair's middle and rested her head in the crook of Blair's arm. Blair tightened her grip just enough to say she had noticed and was content. Because she was. Having the chance to spend time with Ali like this was just priceless. She thought of Susan and hoped she really would be happy for them if this worked out. After all, it was her idea in the first place.

"Thank you for doing this with me." Ali spoke quietly as she tilted her head to gaze up at Blair, her fingers stroking gently back and forth along Blair's left side. She could feel the intake of breath her touch had caused for Blair, and she liked it.

"It's been a really nice time Ali, and it's not over yet!"

Ali turned a little more and raised up on her elbow. "You're right." She leant forward and placed a gentle peck on Blair's lips. "Let's go and get something to eat. We need an early night so we can enjoy tomorrow."

"Tomorrow? You've planned that too?"

"Well, I have an idea of somewhere to go, yes. Is that ok?" A sudden attack of nervousness wiggled its way in and caused Ali to be concerned she was being too pushy with Blair.

"Everything is okay, Ali." She kissed the side of her head and then pushed her gently away so she could get up. Lying there with Ali was doing things to her that she had already promised wouldn't happen until Ali was ready, but she was so ready and she needed space, time, and a little distance to get her arousal back under control.

~***~

Walking into the small eatery was one of those TV moments where everyone in the place stopped what they were doing and turned to see who had wandered into 'their' restaurant.

It was the only one in town, so they didn't have much choice about where they would eat, not that it bothered either woman as they only had eyes for each other right now.

It was in need of a little work but was quaint all the same, and they were shown to a small table in the corner that was cosy, intimate. They ordered a starter and some beer, chatting easily about the day and the weekend in general. Ali found it just as easy as she always had; somehow Blair had that way about her, which she supposed was what made her so good at her job: being able to talk to people and put them at ease.

Blair was smitten and trying desperately not to push Ali too far, but she was finding it difficult not to gush about how she felt when sat with Ali like this. She wanted to tell her how much she loved the way Ali expressed herself with her hands, how she wanted to reach out and stroke her fingers down her cheek and gently tilt her chin towards her own waiting mouth, or how beautiful she looked in a blue dress that matched her eyes almost exactly hue for hue, but instead she sat silently listening as Ali talked so enthusiastically about Vegas and the time she had visited previously with Susan, then rambled about how Blair was so very brave getting a tattoo. Suddenly she was aware that Ali was no longer speaking. Instead she found her looking at her expectantly.

"I'm sorry, what?" Blair asked, understanding instantly that Ali must have asked her something.

"You ok? You kinda zoned out there for a minute." Ali was smiling at her, and it was the most beautiful sight she had seen all day.

"Yes, I am. I am more than ok." She looked around at their surroundings. "Do you wanna get out of here?" Blair asked, taking a breath and sighing. "Because I really just...I just want to be with you. Without the audience." She laughed, looking around once more at the other diners, who were still intrigued with the new arrivals' attendance.

Ali reached out her hand, and Blair wasted no time in taking it, allowing herself to be led from their seats to the front desk, where Ali paid the bill.

As they were leaving Ali stopped them abruptly. Remembering something from her bucket list, she quickly turned around.

"Um, give me one minute," she said, holding one finger up to illustrate just how fast she would be. Intrigued but willing to be patient as always, Blair waited as Ali scampered back inside the diner. She watched as Ali spoke to the young woman who had served them their meal. Ali was still speaking to her as she handed something over, at which point the young woman looked as though she screamed and jumped in the air with excitement before flinging her arms around Ali. They shared a few more words and then Ali was back on the sidewalk next to Blair.

"What did you say to that girl?" Blair asked, needing to know what she had done to make her so happy.

"I remembered something on my bucket list," was all Ali said as she began to smile, her hand automatically slipping into Blair's, their fingers locking around one another as they walked.

"Ok, you keep your secrets." Blair giggled, giving her hand a little squeeze of contentment.

"Oh, it isn't a secret, I just feel a little embarrassed." Which was ridiculous, she thought to herself as she said it, this was Blair. "I gave her a $100 tip."

~***~

Back at the hotel as they got ready for bed, Ali couldn't help but consider that maybe Susan was watching over them, nudging them along. She thought of Susan often, but if she was honest, there were now times when Susan wasn't on her mind quite as much as she used to be. Somewhere along the line these past few months, Blair had sneaked in, and Ali often found herself thinking about the gorgeous blonde.

If you had asked Ali a year ago what she would think about that, the answer would have been quite simple: she wouldn't be thinking of that. But here she was nearly 18 months after Susan passed, considering beginning again, with Blair. It didn't hurt quite as much as it used to.

And if the truth be told, she wanted to sleep with her. Every physical urge to have sex was well and truly present. She couldn't ignore it; her arousal levels spiked whenever Blair was around nowadays. But, something held her back. Not hurting Blair was part of it, but there was something more: Susan. Even though she had Susan's permission, something in the back of her mind still hung on to the idea that she was cheating.

She needed to get over that. She was doing okay on the kissing and cuddling; maybe she just needed to do that more often.

The bathroom door was ajar. Blair stood in front of the sink, brushing her teeth in the mirror. Her hair was tied back and she was already wearing her pyjamas. She looked cute.

"Blair?" Ali asked, walking towards the bathroom.

"Yeah, honey," Blair said without thinking. She stopped brushing the instant that she realised what she had said. "Uh..." She spat quickly and rinsed her mouth.

Ali giggled and leant against the doorjamb. "It's ok, I like it." She smiled.

"Yeah? Ok, great." She wiped her face with a towel. "So, uh?" Ali was staring at her, still smiling.

"Oh, right yeah...So, I was wondering if maybe..." She laughed at what she was about to suggest. "Immersion therapy."

"Uh huh."

"I think it would help me if...can we just kiss, a lot?!"

"Kiss? Oh, I think we can definitely do that," she said edging closer to Ali. She slid her arms around her waist and drew her close. "If that's what you want...I know I won't have any complaints." Their lips met, caressing each other slowly.

"Yeah, I want that," Ali murmured before continuing to immerse herself in Blair.

Chapter Twenty-Eight

Monday morning came too quickly, but Ali was in the office as usual at 7 a.m. Only this time she wasn't sitting in her chair feeling miserable or trying to find something to do to keep her mind busy; in fact, her mind was alive with thoughts. She was thinking of Blair, of the weekend that had been such a success that she was still smiling.

Glancing up at the frame that held a copy of Susan's letter, she stood and walked over to it. She read the words once more and reached out a hand, her fingers lightly touching the glass that held it safely.

"I'm trying to keep my promise, baby," she said aloud, as though speaking to Susan herself. "I get the feeling that you would be happy that Blair is here. She is trying very hard to make me happy, and she does…" She looked up at the ceiling and then back down at the letter. "This is what you wanted, isn't it?" It was a question she still needed an answer to, to feel comfortable with knowing that she wasn't disrespecting their marriage, their life together.

*"I want you to be happy Ali, I want you to meet someone and let them make you happy. That's what I want Ali. Don't feel guilty or miserable for wanting that too."*

She heard Susan's words repeat themselves in her head. She had remembered them before, she remembered everything Susan had said, only now, now she understood it. Now she realised just how much Susan had loved her, loved her enough to let someone else love her too.

~***~

When Jack arrived at eight just like clockwork, he found her in the kitchen, coffee made and pastries laid out like a cake lover's paradise.

"Did I forget someone's birthday?" he asked, a look of anguish on his face as his brain tried to file through the information it stored in order to work out who he had forgotten. Because if it was Ola, then he was really in trouble. He couldn't risk losing out on all that delicious food she cooked for everyone.

"No, I just thought you all deserved something nice," Ali answered, putting him out of his misery just as Paula and Ola wandered in too.

"Oh, birthday?"

"No." Ali laughed this time. "Can someone not just buy cakes around here?"

"Nope, not if I am going to keep my hips this size," Paula countered with a wicked grin.

"Oh please girl, your hips are just fine!" Ola argued, bumping her hip against the one in question.

"Well, in that case, you better pass me over that really big chocolate one right there." She pointed it out to Ola, who grabbed it and passed it right over.

Once Fi and Sara had arrived and all of them had enjoyed the unexpected breakfast provided, Ali called a meeting. Inquisitive looks and questions were shared with the group as they wondered why, but one by one they did as they were asked and filed into the conference room to take their seats at the table.

Ali stood at the front of the room in front of the seat that she always sat in. She took her suit jacket off and hung it on the back of her chair, revealing a white shirt that was unbuttoned halfway down her chest, the sleeves rolled neatly, showing off her tanned arms. She wore a navy pencil skirt that matched the jacket and heels. She looked every inch a professional, but they could all notice the difference: Ali was relaxed. She was smiling and seemed happier than they had seen her in a long time.

"I wanted to take a moment to thank you all, not just for the last week or so and getting us through the difficult couple of accounts we had but, well..." She looked around at them all. Each one of them had been there for her, made her life easier; taken on more than they were required or expected to. "The last year and more, as you all know, has been difficult for me, and I know at times I made life difficult for you all too." She smiled an acknowledgement as they all attempted to disagree. She raised her hand and continued. "It's true, there have been times I have been hard to work for, and you all know it. All of you could have walked away at any point but you didn't, you all stuck with me, and without you all I wouldn't have gotten through this, so I just wanted to take this time to make sure you all know that I am thankful, I am grateful for each and every one of you."

"Ali, we wouldn't have it any other way." Paula spoke for them all with her words as they each nodded in agreement. "We all loved Susan, not as much as you did we can admit." There were smiles and giggles around the room. "But we did, we lost her too, we weren't going to lose you as well."

"Thank you. But this is supposed to be me thanking you guys!" she laughed. "So, thank you." She checked her watch, picked up her bag and grabbed her coat as they all watched. "I'm going to take the rest of the day off." She grinned, pulling her car keys from her bag. "Paula, you're in charge." She laughed as the rest of them groaned.

~***~

By ten a.m., Blair was in full swing at the office. She had rosters to organise, and the entertainment program for the following month had fallen on her shoulders until she could interview and employ someone to take charge of it on a more full-time basis. She didn't mind so much; it was a lot of fun organising musicians and small theatre companies to come in and entertain the residents. She had even managed to sign up a local potter and ceramic artist who would come in and spend time with residents to make vases and various other small items from clay.

They were not fully filled as yet, but with 23 guests, they had enough to keep them busy. In many ways Blair was glad of that for now; it gave all of the staff a little more time to settle and find their feet.

The time flew by without Blair taking much notice until the clock struck two p.m. There was a sharp knock against her door, and with no organised appointments on her agenda, she wondered briefly who it could be. There was a hope there that it might be another impromptu visit from Ali. A smile graced her lips in anticipation.

"Hey, how are – oh, Josie!" The blonde nurse was surprised to see the woman she had been dating on and off standing in her office; she had never shown any interest in visiting previously.

"Hi, I was in the neighbourhood and—" Josie was a shorter woman, curvy in all the right places. She had a new pixie cut to her hair, and Blair thought it suited her much better than the previous style she had worn.

"Right, come in, I'm sorry, where are my manners? Come in." She took a step backwards, opening the door wider for Josie to enter. "So, how have you been?"

"Oh, you know, pretty well. You?" She watched as Blair walked towards her desk and perched on the edge of it.

"Actually, pretty busy really, a lot to get done around here."

"I can imagine. I haven't heard from you in a while so..." She moved closer, her eyes searching Blair's face.

"I'm sorry..." There was a knock at the door again. This time Blair called out and the door opened in an instant.

"Sorry Miss Barnes, but when you're finished could you pop upstairs and speak to Jonathon's parents?" Lisa, one of her most experienced nurses, requested.

"Absolutely, I'll be right up, I am sorry Josie, do you mind?"

"Of course not, maybe we can catch up over dinner tonight?" she asked, not caring that Lisa was still in the room with them.

"Uh Lisa, if you could wait for me outside," she requested, waiting for her employee to leave the room. She needed to make things clear with Josie about how her life had changed recently. "Actually Josie, I am kind of seeing someone right now, and I'm in love with her. I thought you and I were—"

"Just fun? Of course, I am happy for you Blair. We had fun and that's all it was." She smiled and walked forward. Closing the space between them, she placed a kiss on the corner of Blair's mouth just as the door opened once more. Only this time it was Ali, and her face looked like thunder.

"Ali?" Blair began, but stopped the moment she realised speaking wasn't going to solve anything right now.

"Well, I guess your nurse was right after all," Ali seethed, looking back over her shoulder down the corridor at the back of

Lisa. "You're with your girlfriend." And with that she turned and left the room, slamming the door behind her as she went.

"I see, and that would be her I take it?" Josie said, unsure of exactly what had just happened.

The phone rang and Blair grabbed it, listening as the person on the other end explained something, and then she placed it down gently.

"I'm sorry, I need to go, one of my patients is very close to death and I need to—" She needed to go to Ali too, but she couldn't walk away while Jonathon needed her. "I need to see to Jonathon."

Chapter Twenty-Nine

There was an amazing storm raging, not just outside but within Ali herself. The sky had darkened to an amalgam of grey that stretched across the horizon for as far as the eye could see, the clouds scurrying from left to right as the wind picked up and blew its violent rage. Leaves and trash whipped up and danced together down the street, caressing one another as they went.

Ali found her thoughts much the same, dancing violently with her feelings. She liked Blair, really liked her. She wanted so much to just be able to enjoy the time they spent together, just as she had found a way to justify her feelings and not feel guilty about Susan. She realised how stupid it had been now to place all of her emotional trust in the hands of someone who was still seeing somebody else, and she was angry with herself. She had known all about Josie. She assumed that was who was with Blair in her office, though who knew, maybe Blair had more than two women on the go. It didn't matter anymore. She was done with it all. She had Susan; it might only be a memory now, but it was a whole lot better than the feeling she had right at this moment. Anger.

*"Do you have all the facts baby?"* Susan asked, as Ali paced the living room, angry.

*"Of course, isn't it obvious? How stupid can I be?"*

*"Ali, you're not stupid. You wanted to believe in someone and they let you down, they let YOU down baby, it isn't a reflection on you."*

*"Isn't it? I should have listened to my guts."*

She had left Blair's office and had intended to drive straight home, only she hadn't ended up there. She had driven to the cemetery, and in the failing light, she had wandered the gravestones until she found Susan's headstone. She slumped down against it, her heart in pieces as she sobbed.

It was only the darkness falling that had woken her, the cold air of night seeping into her pores and bones. Curled up in a ball on top of the grave, she had cried herself to sleep with exhaustion. Her body ached, and she was cold and stiff. Numb, physically and mentally.

Her phone was dead, the battery long since given up. Her clothes were damp from the evening's drizzle. She staggered to her feet and finally made it home before the storm broke. The rain pelted down, slamming into the windows before dripping downwards like a river of precipitation, the wind whipping up as her world crashed down around her.

Loud banging on the door brought her out of her reverie. A fist was pounding hard and urgently. She stomped across the hallway towards the door and flung it open, ready to tell whoever it was that was attempting to bother her that right now wasn't a good time.

Blair stood outside in the rain dripping wet, her long blonde hair plastered to her head as the water cascaded down to her not-so-waterproof jacket. The sight of her tugged at a multitude of emotions. She wanted to pull her into an embrace, slap her, kiss her in the rain, and tell her to leave all at once. Anger won out.

"Just go home Blair," she advised, pushing the door to close it.

"No, not until you listen to me," she replied, placing her palm against the door, teeth chattering from the cold. The wind whipped around her, her hair flying around her face as she tried desperately to convince Ali to hear her out.

"I don't want to hear it, ok? Just go!" she shouted, closing the door. Her forehead rested against the dark wood as she breathed in deeply and tried to stop the tears that had begun to fall without her even noticing.

"I'm not leaving!" Blair called from the other side of the door as Ali turned and slid down to the floor, sobbing her heart out once more. "I'm not going anywhere Ali, because you're wrong, you're wrong about me," Blair continued.

Thunder rocked the sky. Moments later lightning lit the hallway and caused Ali to flinch. The rain pounded against the windows and the wind continued to hammer, matching the cadence of her heartbeat. She didn't know how long she sat there for, but it was darker now. She moved away from the door and stretched out her legs before standing.

"Ali?" Blair was cold now. Her clothes were soaked, but she wasn't going to leave. "Ali, please." Her teeth chattered and she was shivering. "You have to listen to me," she begged quietly.

The door opened slowly. Ali stood in the opening looking down at the sorrowful sight of Blair sitting on the ground like she had been washed up on the shore following a flood.

"You should go home, Blair." Ali's voice had softened, but the anger still lingered. Her face was hard as stone as she looked away and out into the distance.

"No." Blair shook her head, droplets of water flicking and falling as she pulled herself to her feet. She stuttered and shivered. "I can't, I can't walk away while you think something about me that is wrong, so, so wrong Ali." She took a step forward, and when Ali didn't move she kept moving forward until Ali finally stepped aside and let her into the house. Water immediately pooled around her feet as she stood shivering and shaking. The coldness had enveloped her a while ago; what she felt now went far beyond the cold.

"I...that was J-J-Josie, who you saw me with, Lisa heard her ask me to have dinner with her, b-b-but she left the room before she heard me t-t-tell her I couldn't because I w-w-was-." She continued to shiver and stutter as she tried to get the words out. "Because I w-w-was in l-l-love with someone."

Ali stood still, watching her, trying to read her, knowing in her heart that she believed her. She remembered all the conversations, all the times they had spent together, and knew that Blair was telling the truth, because Blair was better than that. She knew the blonde in front of her, she knew her! She knew the kind of person she was.

"You love me?" she said, unable to stop her fingers from reaching forward and placing Blair's hair behind her ear before cupping her wet, cold cheek. She was freezing.

"Yes." She nodded as best she could. The trembling continued as Ali pulled Blair against her and held her tight, her wet clothing soaking through Ali's own clothes.

"You're drenched," she said, more to herself than to Blair.

"I f-f-figured I'd give you some space, but w-w-when the ph-ph-phone was still off this evening I decided to drive over. Th-th-then I got a flat and I h-had to walk the last mile or so," she explained as Ali unzipped her coat and began pulling it off her, dragging it down wet arms. It gripped the skin and refused to budge until she tugged a little more; desperate to get her warm again. She was only wearing a flimsy t-shirt underneath, and it was soaked through too. Ali dumped the jacket on the floor and began to pull the top from where it was stuck, tucked inside her jeans. Blair was shivering, and it worried Ali.

"You should have gone home!" Ali insisted as she began to unbutton her jeans and yank them down her cold, damp thighs. Blair leant her weight against Ali as she felt the jeans being tugged around her ankles, lifting each leg one by one so Ali could pull them free. She felt lightheaded and wobbled on her feet.

The overwhelming need to care for this woman becoming the all-consuming thought in Ali's mind as she continued to listen.

"I couldn't, n-n-not while y-y-you thought s-s-so badly of me." Blair shivered, her teeth chattering a little more. "The storm, it's—"

"Yes, it's bad. Come on, you need to warm up." She pulled her by the hand and led her to the bathroom in just her underwear. She hit the on switch and the shower started to pump warm water within seconds, steam beginning to fill the cold air of the room.

Blair's shivering continued as her breathing became more rapid. She could barely hold herself up, and she was so pale. Ali held her up against the tiled wall with one palm pressed against her chest. While she was supported, she quickly stripped out of her own clothes until she stood in her underwear too. Helping Blair into the cubicle and closing the door, she held her under the warm water and let the steam build up round them. She kept their bodies flush against one another, her own body heat helping to warm Blair as her hands moved up and down her back, stimulating the blood flow.

"I would never do that to you, Ali," Blair stuttered against her ear.

"I know, try not to speak, you need to get warm."

With the colour returning to Blair's cheeks and the shivering subsiding, Ali figured it was safe to get out of the water and dry her off. Removing the last vestige of clothing, she tried not to study Blair's nakedness, but it was impossible to ignore. Blair was someone she couldn't ignore, beautiful in every way. She was physically different to Susan in almost every way, and Ali was beginning to understand that that was okay. Blair was never going to be Susan, or be better than Susan, or replace Susan, and that was okay too.

~***~

They were in bed, naked. She was still wrapped around Blair, skin on skin as her body heat transferred to that of the woman in her bed, Susan's bed. Their bed. Blair was sleeping, tangled limbs and arms wrapped around one another, the duvet pulled up to her neck. It was warm, comfortable, and as Ali took a deep breath and exhaled, she felt the presence of her wife. She felt the words in her heart as they echoed through her head, and she heard Susan clear as day.

*"It's okay, my love. Be happy, let your heart open its doors."*

She pulled Blair tighter to her, kissed the top of her head, and felt her begin to stir. She mumbled something that Ali couldn't quite understand, so she just smiled and rubbed her palm soothingly up and down her naked spine.

Sleepy Blair was cute. The smile on to her face continued to grow as brown warm eyes slowly focused and began to lazily smile too as she realised that everything must be okay or at the very least, be heading that way.

The storm was still raging outside. Thunderous claps shook the windows, followed by a bright striking light that lit up the room around them, but it had calmed inside of Ali. The rage she had felt at the unfairness of life had moved on, the rainfall of tears had ceased, and the only thing lighting up her mind right now was the woman in her arms.

"Am I naked in your bed?" Blair asked quizzically, with a hint of humour as she pulled back enough to look at Ali.

"Oh, yeah. Completely naked and in my bed," Ali offered in return. Blair nodded as she considered this news. "So, are you feeling better?"

"I feel much warmer now yes, thank you." She snuggled back in, indulging in the moment, enjoying the skin-on-skin feeling as her arm slid effortlessly around Ali's waist.

"Blair?" Ali's voice was quiet, almost a whisper. She waited for Blair to look at her once more, to acknowledge with her own eyes what Ali was about to convey.

As Blair raised her head, she saw the smile and smiled back, knowing that this had become Ali's way of initiating intimacy. Shy and yet completely genuine was how Blair viewed that smile. There was no time to think, to consider. Ali brought her mouth to Blair's and kissed her lips, gently nudging them with her own until

Blair began to kiss back. It was reverent but passionate, explorative and yet knowing. Tempting and teasing.

This time as Blair's hands began to move, Ali reciprocated without thought, without guilt. She moved her own palms slowly against the warm flesh beneath them, relaxing into the feeling of being touched, of touching. Her palm slid effortlessly down Blair's bare back until she reached the contour of her ass and squeezed the fleshy globe. She felt the same movement from Blair and then anticipated the way Blair's hand moved around between them and smoothed its way up her stomach, enjoying the contours of her stomach until it found a breast to caress and enfold. Ali felt her nipple strain and stiffen under the touch and couldn't suppress the gasp and subsequent moan that escaped her throat as Blair moved her mouth from her lips and began to descend her neck. She sucked and licked a path that triggered all her nerve endings to burst with some kind of electrical pulse that surged through her and connected her to the woman currently exploring with her veneration and subtlety. Fingers moved constantly, wanting to touch every inch of her, never pausing as they moved on, this time downward. Her mouth replaced her fingers where they had tweaked and teased, equally as teasing now as the warmth of her mouth tenderly encompassed her nipple. Ali felt herself moving, being turned onto her back as Blair raised herself higher to hover above her. Their eyes met and locked.

"Are you sure?" Blair whispered, so close to Ali's ear that her breath sent a shiver through her. She felt her nod, but moved to gaze at her face once more to see for herself that this was really what Ali wanted too. She found the answer right there in the blue eyes that had darkened with arousal, in the silent nod of want.

In that one single moment, she saw everything she needed to see: the woman she had been slowly falling in love with finally at peace with her feelings. As she brought their mouths together once more, she reached her hand between them and found her, explored her with teasingly slow movements, learning her, reading her, and working her until she heard the quiet moan and the voice that pleaded for more. Every curve of her led somewhere enticing, exciting, and under the fading light of the storm, she found herself able to see so much more clearly.

She felt Ali's firm thigh move slowly between her own, her own need and want evident as she slid back and forth, her hips beginning to move with their own volition. Thunder pounded as once again the storm returned. The blonde teased her fingers at the entrance to her lover before tenderly moving inside of her, rocking into her with the same rhythm of her hips as they undulated beneath her. The iridescent glare of a lightning strike lit up her features. Revelling in the desire to fulfil, she concentrated harder, listened, felt and witnessed every soft moan, every twitch of muscle, every breath, and memorised it.

They moved together as one. Ali felt the all-too-familiar sensations building low in the pit of her stomach and deep within her core at the ministrations, her lover bringing her slowly to the precipice of a wanton desire to find the release as the thunder crashed, nearer again this time. Rain pelted the window in a continuous pattern. She felt the slickness of her lover against her flesh as Blair kept up with her in every way, building together to bring themselves a shared gratification she had denied herself for so long. Blair's hips rocked unconsciously faster as her fingers kept rhythm, and then she cried out and arched, her body stiffening, every muscle and sinew striving to eke out every last ounce of pleasure she could share.

The sight of Blair succumbing to her body's needs drove Ali over her own edge as she gripped her tightly, her body shaking and shuddering with the vibrations of pleasure.

They rolled together and clung to one another as aftershocks gently shivered through them both.

~***~

Dinner had been a mismatch of salad and cheese. The power had gone out at some point earlier in the evening, when both women had been too involved with each other to notice.

There had been no let-up in the weather. The downpour continued to saturate everything in its path. Ali stood at the sink washing the plates, watching the rain from the window. The wind gusted across the lawn, blowing everything out of its way, including the rain, as it pushed the droplets into the glass with a hard tap, tap, tap.

Blair moved in quietly behind her, wrapping her arms around her waist as she rested her chin in the crook of her neck. With a subtle kiss, she exhaled.

"Hey," she whispered, with another peck of warm lips against her ear that made Ali squirm and giggle. She grabbed the dish towel and dried her hands before turning in the arms around her. Blair didn't move, keeping their bodies flush against one another as she tilted her head and kissed the perfectly pouting lips in front of her.

"Hi." Blair reached for her hands and led her backwards from the kitchen across to the living room. There were lanterns and candles lit all around the room, the darkness of the storm eclipsed by the numerous tiny flames that jittered and danced. She had lit the fire, several logs now burning hard in the grate, and she had found all the blankets still in the same cupboard they had always been in while she had lived here. They were scattered on the floor, a cosy nesting spot.

"Oh my God, Blair!" she gasped, looking around the room. "It's beautiful in here."

"Yes, it is," she said, pulling her down to the floor with her. "Let's talk."

"Talk? Okay..." They both sat facing one another, cross-legged and holding hands across their laps.

"So, you okay?" Blair asked, her thumbs rubbing gently across the back of Ali's hands.

Ali took a deep breath, bit her bottom lip, and smiled. "I am really okay. Thank you, for being patient and not giving up on me."

"Why on Earth would I give up on you, Susan would haunt me till my dying day." She laughed and Ali joined in; she really could see her wife doing that. "Ya know, she knew this would happen?"

"Ya think?"

"Oh, I know, she used to tell me all the time." Blair grinned. "Of course, I took no notice of her. She was mischievous, that one."

Ali nodded again. "Yes, she was."

"I want to be completely honest with you, no secrets between us." Blair spoke with a sincerity that Ali liked. "You weren't the only person Susan had make her a promise. I made one too."

Ali tilted her head, intrigued by this new titbit of information.

"Apparently, I wasn't that great at hiding my crush on you." She blushed, and Ali stifled a grin. "In fact, Susan used to enjoy herself at my expense a lot." Blair chuckled at the memory.

"She never told me."

"Of course not. You would have had me out of here in a heartbeat."

"That's true, I was looking for any excuse to get rid of you in the beginning, but then you kind of grew on me." She leant forward and kissed her quickly. She liked that she could do that now.

"So, when we got back from the beach, she had me make a promise."

"What did she make you promise?" Ali twisted around and sat in Blair's lap. Blair opened her legs and allowed it, wrapping her arms around her. She kissed the back of her head before Ali sank back against her.

"I promised that when the time was right, I would help you to move forward, so that you could get to a place where you could let somebody love you."

Ali was quiet for a moment, and Blair worried for a second that this was information overload for Ali. "And you kept your promise, just like I did," Ali said, her voice quiet and reverent. "Susan loved me, and I loved her, that won't ever change, but she was right about everything. She always did know what was best for me." She twisted around to face Blair.

"She loved you so much, and I promise, I am going to do all I can to make you happy." Their eyes met and held before she added, "I love you, Ali."

"I know you do, and I am going to let you." She leant forward and kissed her gently on the lips. "Because I've fallen in love with you, too."

The Promise

# ABOUT THE AUTHOR

Claire Highton-Stevenson has previously published two books in the Cam Thomas Serial. OUT and NEXT.
She lives in Sussex with her wife, two cats and two dogs.
Claire is an avid Liverpool FC fan and is often found out and about with her camera.
An active member of social media. You can get in contact via Facebook, Twitter or Instagram by following ItsClaStevOffical.